THE **HARDY BOYS**®

#170
KICKOFF TO DANGER

FRANKLIN W. DIXON

A MINSTREL®
BOOK

Published by POCKET BOOKS
New York London Toronto Sydney Singapore

For information regarding special discounts for bulk purchases, please
contact Simon & Schuster Special Sales at 1-800-456-6798 or
business@simonandschuster.com

This book is a work of fiction. Names, characters, places and incidents are
products of the author's imagination or are used fictitiously. Any resemblance
to actual events or locales or persons, living or dead, is entirely coincidental.

A MINSTREL PAPERBACK *Original*

A Minstrel Book published by
POCKET BOOKS, a division of Simon & Schuster, Inc.
1230 Avenue of the Americas, New York, NY 10020

ISBN: 0-7434-0685-0

First Minstrel Books printing November 2001

10 9 8 7 6 5 4 3 2 1

THE HARDY BOYS MYSTERY STORIES is a trademark
of Simon & Schuster, Inc.

THE HARDY BOYS, A MINSTREL BOOK and colophon
are registered trademarks of Simon & Schuster, Inc.

Printed in the U.S.A.

Contents

KICKOFF TO DANGER

1 Saved by the Bell

Frank Hardy looked up in surprise when the end-of-class buzzer went off. He hadn't been watching the clock. All his attention had been focused on the math problem covering most of the chalkboard.

Others in the class felt saved by the bell. Relieved sighs filled the air as kids began pulling their books together.

"We'll come back to this problem tomorrow," Mr. Patel, the math instructor, said. "For tonight, review chapter five. The secret to cracking this problem is in there." He turned to write on the board. "Also, work on problems three, seven, eleven, twelve, fifteen, and nineteen. If you can't do those tomorrow, I'll know you haven't read the chapter."

Frank scribbled down the assignment and got

1

his books. As he headed for the door, Callie Shaw joined him.

"I almost thought we'd escape without homework," she said.

"Fat chance," Frank replied with a grin. "Even if it's the last class of the day, Patel isn't going to let anyone rush him."

"I don't know how he does it," Callie said, glancing back through the door. Frank followed her gaze. Their teacher, neat as ever, was erasing the board before he left.

"He's a quiet little guy, but nobody ever steps out of line in his class." Callie rolled her big, blue eyes. "Unlike Mr. Weak."

Mr. Weak, whose real name was Mr. Weeks, was Bayport High's new English instructor. This was his first year teaching, and his inexperience showed. His class could best be described as a zoo.

"It's a shame he can't keep a few people quiet," Frank said. "It ruins things for everybody."

"Yeah—too bad nobody stirs things up in math class, instead." Callie gave Frank a mischievous smile. "If I get another of those questions about the speed of a car . . ."

She shook her head until her blond hair swirled around her face.

"You need trigonometry if you're going to be a physicist," Frank said seriously.

"Exactly how I plan to spend my future career."

2

Callie burst into laughter at the look on Frank's face.

"Hey, not *everybody* is a tech genius, you know." She reached out and ruffled his dark hair. "Speaking of tech geniuses, how's it going with that brain-busting college course you're taking?"

"It's a challenge," Frank admitted, "and a rush. This isn't just a computers for dummies course. College *seniors* are taking this sucker. And I'm not treated like some punk kid who got in by mistake. They really listen to me."

"Why wouldn't they?" Callie wanted to know. She patted Frank on the arm. "Sounds like you're enjoying yourself."

"In a frazzled kind of way." Frank looked at his watch. "Nobody's going to be listening to me if I don't get to the university." He looked at Callie. "Especially if I'm going to give you a lift home."

Callie laughed. "Then let's move it, Hardy."

They stopped off at her locker, then at Frank's. Finally they made their way out a side door in the south wing of the school.

Frank had passed over Bayport High in a plane several times. Seen from above, the school looked like a giant capital *E* lying on its side. The back of the *E* was the original high school, built in the 1930s. With its red brick and central tower, the building looked like Independence Hall.

Frank had been to Philadelphia and knew that

3

Bayport High was much larger than the national landmark. The school stretched two blocks long and almost two blocks deep with the additions that had been made over the years. The south wing, added in the sixties, had made the school look like an *L*. Next came the north wing in the eighties. Frank could remember when the middle stroke of the *E* had been added. That section held offices, a new gym, and locker rooms. A loading dock jutted out from the rear of the gym, with faculty parking on either side. Then came the paved expanse of student parking, and beyond that the sports fields.

Frank had parked on a side street north of the school, hoping to escape the dismissal traffic jam. To reach his van, he and Callie would have to cut across the parking lot, passing one athletic field.

As they did, the gym door banged open, and the football team headed out for practice. The guys were hustling along. One clown actually came out on the loading dock and jumped down to the pavement. Frank slowed up, watching his former teammates run past.

Callie slipped an arm through Frank's. "Do you miss not going out for the team this year?" she asked.

Frank shook his head. "I couldn't turn down the computer class, once I got in," he said. "Besides, Eddie Taplinger is just as good a quarterback as I was."

4

Still, he didn't move from the fence as the team broke into squads for different practice sessions. The defensive linemen began setting up tackling sleds. Eddie Taplinger stood tossing a football in one hand, while the running backs took off down the field.

"I think Joe misses me on the team more than I miss football," Frank said with a laugh. The Hardy brothers had made a good passing team in other seasons.

There was no missing his younger brother's short-cropped blond hair. Joe raised a hand as he charged down the field, yelling to Eddie to throw the ball his way.

Callie nodded. "Especially since that new kid joined the team."

"Terry Golden?" Frank shifted his eyes to another kid in a Bayport uniform. He was blond, like Joe, but he wore his hair longer. Golden was maybe an inch taller than Joe, Frank's height, and carrying a little more muscle.

"They're starting to treat him like he *is* golden," Callie said.

"He helped the team start the season with three wins out of three," Frank pointed out. "It's kind of hard to argue with victory."

"Not to mention that he matched Joe's record ball return," Callie said.

"And in the very first game he played for Bay-

5

port." Frank shrugged. "The guy is good." He looked for a moment into the stands. "In fact, I suspect he's already being scouted by college teams."

Callie stared at him. "You think so?"

"If you ask me, it's going on right now." Frank nodded toward a man sitting high in the concrete grandstand. He balanced a briefcase across his knees to act as a desk for the pad on which he was writing.

"That guy up there is taking notes, and Coach Devlin hasn't asked him to leave." The coach was talking with the team manager, both of whom could see the figure in the stands. Neither seemed to mind his being there.

"I can't imagine the coach letting anyone see the team practicing plays." Frank shook his head. "Not unless it would benefit one of his players."

"You really think some college is trying to sign up Terry Golden?" Callie watched Golden catch a pass from Eddie Taplinger. "Would he be leaving Bayport High?"

Frank shrugged. "Pro teams recruit right out of high school," he said. "Colleges have to wait for graduation."

"So we'll still have the golden one to win games for us," Callie said.

Frank winced at the nickname as he watched the new star send the ball flying back to the quarterback.

6

"Unfortunately," Frank added, "Joe'll have to live with being the second-best pass receiver."

"If *you* were the quarterback, you could cut Joe a break." Callie gave Frank a sly smile. "And what about me? I liked dating a football hero."

Frank responded with a long look. "Well, then, maybe you should talk with what's-his-face—the golden one," he suggested.

"I *have* talked with him," Callie said. "He made me feel as if I should say 'thank you' for the honor."

Before Frank could answer, Callie pointed to the field. "Look! Eddie's finally throwing one to Joe!"

The quarterback launched a long, high pass down the field. Looking over his shoulder, Joe broke into a run, aiming for where the ball would land.

Movement on the other side of the field caught Frank's eye. Terry Golden suddenly launched into a mad charge, aiming for the same spot.

Callie blew up. "Is he trying to make Joe look bad?"

"Golden may be pumping it up for the college scout," Frank said. "You've got to give it to him—he's fast." He shook his head. "But his little display may come off as showboating."

Still running, Joe shot a quick look over his shoulder. His eyes were aimed in the air, at the ball, not on the ground, though.

"Joe doesn't see him!" Callie's voice was tight.

"He's still on course for the ball," Frank said. "And Golden is right behind him."

"But, Frank—" Callie cried. "He's not stopping!"

The football came spiraling down. Joe raised his arms to catch it. Behind him, Terry Golden came pounding up.

There was no way Terry could get his hands on the ball. But he would be just in time to ram into Joe. . . .

2 Hard Hitter

One more step, Joe told himself, as he brought his upraised hands together. Perfect catch!

He just managed to get his fingers hooked on the pigskin when what felt like an eighteen-wheeler smashed into his back.

Joe tumbled forward, the ball flying from his grip.

He didn't land flat on his face—not quite. At the last second he managed to get an arm out and break his fall. A quick roll, and he was back on his feet.

The first thing he saw was Terry Golden.

Joe's back throbbed, but the pain was nothing compared to the fury roaring through his brain.

"What—" Joe sucked in some air to keep from

yelling. "What do you think you're doing, Golden? That was my pass."

"Got to keep your eyes open, Hardy. What if I had been a guy from the other team?"

"This is practice!" Joe realized his hands had curled into fists and forced his fingers open again. "We're all supposed to be on the same team here. And I was practicing catching that pass, not broken-field running. What would you say if I clipped you the next time Eddie sent the ball your way?"

"I'd say that would make you a poor sport." Golden smirked at Joe. "And I'm sure the scout up in the stands would think so, too."

Joe glanced at the man up in the top seats. Then he noticed how Terry had placed himself. He was standing so the scout couldn't see the expression on his face, but could plainly see Joe's.

Golden reached out and patted Joe on the shoulder, a picture of good sportsmanship.

"No hard feelings, pal," Terry told him. "We all have to try harder when the stakes are high."

He turned, scooped up the ball, and lobbed it back to Eddie Taplinger.

Joe barely noticed how the rest of practice went. He was too busy trying to control his temper.

It didn't help when Coach Devlin called him aside and tapped him on the head. "Concentrate, Joe." The coach turned to look up into the stands. "This isn't a day to be in a fog."

10

The guys on the team said that Coach Devlin sometimes brought in scouts—or people he said were scouts—to keep the players on their toes.

Joe didn't have to worry about being recruited by a college team. His grades were good enough to get him into most schools. An athletic scholarship would be icing on the cake for him.

No, if scouts were coming around, they probably weren't after Joe Hardy. They were looking over the team's new star—the golden one.

Well, Terry boy can have all the attention he wants, Joe told himself. As long as he stays away from me.

He ran back into practice, hoping to work off his anger with sweat.

At least he got the sweat part right. By the time practice was over, his jersey was soaked. In the locker room Joe peeled off his uniform and jumped into the shower.

He'd just toweled off and put on his pants when three quick raps sounded on the locker room door. A female voice called, "Everybody decent in there?"

Joe took a quick look around. A couple of guys had no shirts on, but it would take more than that to keep Liz Webling from coming in after a story.

"All clear, Liz," he yelled. "Come on in."

Liz was a reporter for the *Beacon*, Bayport High's newspaper. She joked that printer's ink was

in her blood because her dad ran the *Bayport Times*.

As Liz entered, her eyes flicked around the locker room, making sure Joe hadn't invited her in too soon. She carried a notebook and a mini-cassette recorder, just like a professional journalist. Behind her trailed a tall, skinny guy with a camera.

Joe hid a smile. Dan Freeman looks more out of place among the jocks than Liz does, he thought.

Nobody would take the awkward, skinny boy for an athlete. He wrinkled his nose at the stink of sweat and liniment as he stepped in through the door. As he followed Liz, Dan managed to stumble but did recover before falling flat on his face.

Dan Freeman not only worked for the *Beacon*, he had also made the front page the week before. The Bayport High debate team had scored well at the year's first big tournament, and Dan's brilliant arguments had played a big part in that success.

"The big game against Seneca Tech is coming up," Liz said to Joe. "How do you think we'll do?"

"That's still a week away," Joe answered as Liz made a beeline for Terry Golden.

"Not when you're working on a school paper," Liz threw back over her shoulder. "This issue will come out right before the game. Just call me the early bird."

12

She stopped and smiled at Terry, who gave her a big smile right back. Golden rubbed his long hair with a towel, then let the towel drop and hang loosely from his shoulders.

"This is my first year at Bayport," he said in reply to Liz's first question. "I can't really talk about the way games went in the past. Everybody tells me that Seneca is the team to beat."

Terry grinned down at Liz. "Well, we've managed to beat every other team we've played this season, and I think we've got the right stuff—and the right guys—to handle Seneca."

Terry Golden's humble act made Joe sick. In front of a microphone or at a pep rally, Golden was always modest, giving credit to the team. On the field, though . . .

Joe's back ached where Golden had rammed into him. He turned away from his teammate to watch Dan Freeman. The photographer was quietly roving around the locker room, shooting pictures of guys at their lockers.

Dan noticed Joe watching him and gave an embarrassed smile. "It's Liz's idea," he said. "She thought it would make a more interesting page than one with the team all lined up in their uniforms."

Joe nodded. "Yeah, that usually ends up looking like a yearbook picture."

"We also got some good shots during your practice, I think."

13

Joe blinked. "Really? I didn't even notice you."

Dan gave a half shrug. "I guess that's the sign of a good photographer." He nodded to Liz, still interviewing Golden. "Your friend Golden sure noticed."

"Don't call him my friend!" The words were out before Joe could stop them.

Dan Freeman stared at Joe in surprise, then looked at Terry again. "Yeah," he finally said. "I could understand that."

Now it was Joe's turn to feel embarrassed. Had Dan seen the stunt that Golden had pulled in practice? Even worse, had he taken a picture of it? "Hotshot Sacks Teammate" . . . that headline would be great for the team's morale.

Joe's thoughts must have shown on his face. Dan Freeman shook his head. "Don't worry," he said. "Liz wants to see Bayport win and Seneca lose. She'll make this a nice, upbeat story."

He glanced at Liz and Terry and said, "It will be fine as long as she doesn't believe everything he says."

After Dan snapped a few more shots, Liz asked him over. "I've got what I came for," Liz said. "Now to get it off the tape and onto some paper. We still need a shot of Terry at his locker. You take care of that, then meet me at the newspaper office. Okay?"

Dan nodded. "Okay."

Liz looked around. "Thanks for the story, guys."

"Thank *you*, Liz," Terry replied, still smiling.

That smile disappeared as soon as Liz Webling was out of the room. Golden sneered at Dan. "You're such a wimp, Freeman. Doing everything some girl tells you. 'Yes, boss. Okay, boss.' " He made his voice higher and squeakier with every word.

"She's the editor," Dan replied, keeping his voice even. "If you don't want me to take your picture—"

"What will you use instead?" Golden interrupted. "An extra-wide shot of Fatso Morton over there?"

Chet Morton had the locker beside Joe's. Joe watched his friend's face go red as Chet pretended to be interested in buttoning his shirt.

"I suppose a camera is about all the equipment a nerd like you can handle." Now Golden was back to insulting Dan Freeman. Still sneering, Terry lounged on the bench in front of his locker. He ran a hand through his long blond hair. "So what will it be? Full face? A profile? Just make sure you get my best side."

"I can't," Freeman replied.

"Why not?"

"Because you're sitting on it."

Terry Golden shot up from the bench, ready to take a swing. Then he staggered back as the camera's flash went off in his face.

15

"That's a pretty good action shot," Dan said. "But I don't think it's what Liz had in mind."

Golden looked ready to tear the camera from Freeman's hands, but he obviously realized that wouldn't look too good. "Just do your job," he growled.

"Fine," Dan replied. "If you'll stand by the locker door . . . Lean back a little . . ."

Terry regained his golden-boy smile.

Dan took a few more pictures, then turned away. "I'd say that'll do," he said, heading for the door.

As Terry stood facing his locker, the room became dead silent.

Except, that is, for the snicker Chet Morton couldn't keep in as he obviously recalled Dan's comment about Terry's best side.

Golden whirled to glare at Chet. "You see something funny, fat boy?"

"I—um—" A little too late Chet realized he'd made himself into a target.

"Maybe you'll think this is funny, too." Golden snatched the damp towel from his shoulders and snapped it like a whip at Chet.

The tip of the towel caught Chet on the arm. "Ow!" he cried, his hand going to the spot.

"Hey, come on—" Joe began.

His protest was cut off by the snap of another towel aimed at Chet. This one was in the hands of Wendell Logan, a hulking linebacker.

16

Worse yet, Wendell was one of Chet's defensive squadmates.

"You think it's funny to have that nerd mouth off to a teammate? I guess we'll have to change your mind."

Logan snapped his towel again, looking around. "Right, guys?"

"Yeah." One of the players leaned past Joe, aiming his towel at Chet, too.

"Count me in," a big tackle said, taking a shot.

Another towel flicked past Joe. Whoever took that shot didn't give any warning.

Chet stumbled away from Joe, trying to avoid the snapping towels. Joe attempted to block him from the guys on his side but got pushed away.

Terry Golden might have a big mouth and ego to match, but his teammates were backing him up. In their eyes, he was one of their own.

Caught against the lockers, Chet took another couple of shots. His face slowly went red. Joe sometimes thought that Chet was too easygoing, that he didn't have the killer instinct needed for football. But Chet could get mad. He grabbed one of the flicking towels and pulled it from his tormentor's hand.

Then another towel snapped in to nail him on the shoulder. When Chet saw who was behind this blow, he dropped his newly seized weapon.

Joe was just as surprised. Biff Hooper had

17

swung on Chet. Biff, who'd been Chet's friend since they were kids!

Chet's face showed a different kind of pain. All the fight went out of him—he just wanted to get away from this. Spinning around, he took a couple of blind steps. The bench set in front of the lockers caught him right beneath the knees. Chet sprawled across it to land on the floor.

Wendell Logan's laughter sounded like an animal's snarl as he came over the bench toward Chet.

Chet must have had the wind knocked out of him because he just lay where he was.

"Brace yourself, fat boy!" Logan gloated as he brought the towel back for another shot.

"I guarantee you—this one's really gonna hurt!"

3 Against the Odds

The instant he heard Wendell Logan's words Joe Hardy moved. He vaulted over the bench and caught hold of the towel behind Wendell's back.

The linebacker started to swing but turned in surprise as the towel was yanked from his grasp.

"That's enough." Joe tossed the towel to the floor.

Wendell Logan bent down, reaching to regain his weapon.

Joe pinned the towel to the floor with his foot. "I said, that's *enough!*"

The big, burly Logan looked around. None of the others on the team had followed him. They were just standing in front of their lockers, staring.

Joe turned to Chet. "Let's get out of here," he said.

Frank Hardy came home after his college class to find his supper waiting on the kitchen table. He pretty much expected that. His mom and aunt Gertrude had gotten used to his new schedule.

What he didn't expect to find was Callie Shaw sitting at the table with his math book.

"I forgot mine," she said, embarrassed. "And I needed to get the problems Mr. Patel assigned."

Frank grinned. "Not to mention a blow-by-blow of what happened to Joe."

Callie looked a little more embarrassed but nodded her head. "I guess Golden was sweet as anything when Liz Webling interviewed him for the school paper, but we saw how rotten he was to Joe on the field," Callie finished. "Everyone's calling him Dr. Golden and Mr. Hyde."

Frank started eating. "Joe can deal with him."

Callie shook her head, her blue eyes troubled. "I'm not worried about you or Joe around this guy. But he's gathering a crew, a gang, and they're beginning to pick on people."

A forkful of food stopped on the way to Frank's mouth. "What people?"

"Ask your brother," Callie said.

Frank put down his fork and went upstairs to Joe's room. Joe sat on the edge of his bed, doing

forearm curls with a dumbbell in time to music from the radio.

That was a bad sign. Joe usually went in for that kind of exercise to work off a bad mood.

"Saw your little run-in with Terry Golden today." Frank expected Joe to complain about being deserted. That's what he'd been saying since Frank had started his computer course and left the team.

Joe only shrugged his shoulders, still working the weight. "I guess he's what people call a necessary evil. We need him to win games, but I don't have to like him."

Joe stopped his exercises and gave Frank a sour smile. "And I suppose it's just as well you got off the team when you did. It's hard enough listening to Eddie Taplinger explain why he passes to Golden instead of me. It would be harder hearing that from my own brother."

Frank felt a little relief when he heard that. "I hear Golden is collecting some sort of crew."

Joe nodded. "Some guys on the team seem to think that if they act like Golden, a little of his success might rub off on them."

"And since he's acting like a real nimrod, so are they?"

"Man, are they!" Joe burst out. "Golden had a run-in with Dan Freeman but ended up looking like a complete jerk. The golden one then tried to

take it out on Chet Morton . . . with lots of help from his crew." Joe frowned. "It was almost like a lynch mob. You wouldn't believe it."

Frank asked, "Don't you think you're being a little too dramatic?"

"How's this for dramatic? Biff Hooper joined in the towel snapping against Chet. He and Chet have been friends since they were kids," Joe said. "B.G.—before Golden."

Frank tried to shrug off the story, but Joe's last line troubled him.

Things only got worse the next morning. Frank and Biff shared an English class along with Dan Freeman and Terry Golden—English, with Mr. Weeks.

Mr. Weeks was having his usual hard time controlling the rowdy kids. But Terry Golden was more than rowdy, he was downright belligerent.

He slammed his poetry book shut. "Why should I be interested in some dusty old sonnet?" Terry challenged the teacher.

"Surprise, surprise, Golden," Dan Freeman spoke up. "There are a few other things to learn besides how to catch a ball."

Golden swung round in his desk as if someone had smacked him. "Typical nerd," he sneered.

"Yeah," Dan replied pleasantly. "It's how this nerd will be accepted at Harvard while you go to

22

some cow college with a major in football. If you're lucky and don't get injured, maybe—*maybe* you'll get a shot at pro ball."

Freeman continued to smile at the fuming jock. "Come to my law office when you're thirty-five and too old to play anymore. You'll need all the help you can get in your new career as a has-been."

Golden scowled. "You think you're smart, Freeman, but all you've got is a smart mouth."

"I'm still looking for *anything* on you that's smart," Dan shot back.

Golden's desk clattered to the floor, knocked over as the jock jumped up.

Mr. Weeks rushed over. "Sit down, Terence."

Terry ignored the order. "I'm going to teach that little snot-nose a lesson."

"You and the rest of what muscle-bound army?" Dan Freeman challenged. He, too, scrambled up out of his seat.

Dan's got nerve, Frank thought. I just hope he's not depending on Mr. Weak to protect him.

Weeks tried to catch Terry Golden's arm as he drew it back to let fly with a punch. Frank shook his head when the teacher missed. There's a useless move. Golden spends every day practicing how to get past guys who want to stop him.

"I want both of you back at your desks—now!"

The stern command would have sounded better if Weeks's voice hadn't cracked.

Terry Golden took another step forward, his arm still cocked.

"You're looking at detention," Weeks warned. "Both of you."

The jock stared at his teacher with scorn. "You think Coach Devlin will let that happen? I'm too important to the team to be sidelined."

"Sit down!" Weeks was now shaking with anger. Frank noticed the teacher wasn't talking about detention anymore.

Terry Golden spread his hands. "Hey, chill out, Mr. *Weak . . . sss.*"

He swaggered back to his desk as if he'd won this round, but the look he sent to Dan Freeman said that the fight was far from over.

Joe Hardy stared at his brother across the cafeteria table. "Did they actually start swinging at each other?" He shook his head in disbelief. "I never get any interesting classes."

"It didn't go that far," Frank admitted. "Not that Mr. Weeks was able to do anything. He threatened Golden with detention but only got laughed at."

Slumped in his seat at the lunch table, Chet Morton didn't say a thing. Frank noticed that Chet was not eating, only playing with the spaghetti on his plate.

Golden must really be getting to him, Frank thought. Mention the guy's name, and Chet loses his appetite.

Joe tried a joke. "Well, with a nickname like Mr. Weak—" He broke off, staring at the lunch line. "Check it out," he muttered.

Terry Golden made his way through the long cafeteria line, cutting in to grab whatever he wanted. He stepped away with his tray as if he were leading a victory parade.

"Yo! Golden!" Wendell Logan called from the table where he sat with a couple of other muscular linemen.

Golden didn't respond to Logan's invitation. Instead, he took his tray to the table the Hardys shared with Chet.

"Join you for a minute?" Golden didn't wait for an answer. He just planted himself at the one empty seat.

Frank watched his brother toss his sandwich down. Golden should rent himself out as a miracle diet, Frank thought. He kills appetites wherever he goes.

Chet, on the other hand, was frozen like a deer caught in headlights.

"So, how do we rate the honor of a lunch visit?" Frank tried to keep his voice light. He wasn't sure he succeeded.

"Hey, I'm not a guy to hang around where he's

not wanted," Terry said. "I only came over because I'm concerned about Chet."

Chet stared at him. "C-concerned?"

"Yeah. I worry about you." Golden gave Chet a big smile. "I couldn't help noticing you had something dangerous on your tray."

"D-dangerous?" Chet began to sound like a stuttering echo. He looked down at his tray as if he expected to find a bomb on it.

Golden pointed to the piece of chocolate cake beside the plate of spaghetti. "I'm talking about that!"

Chet stared, his mouth hanging open.

Terry reached over, grabbed the cake, and stuffed most of it into his mouth. " 'Shad fuh yuh," he said, chewing noisily.

Chet looked as if he didn't believe what was happening.

Frank was having a hard time believing it, too.

Golden scraped chocolate frosting off his hand, using the edge of Chet's tray. "Got to watch that waistline, Chet boy."

He leaned over again. This time he ground his thumb into what was left of Chet's cake.

At last Chet began to come out of his trance. "Hey, you—"

"What are you going to do, fat boy?" Golden's sneer dared Chet to try something. "I've got *teachers* afraid to go up against me." He gave Frank and

Joe a smug grin. "You should think about joining a winner's team."

Laughing, Golden picked up his tray and headed over to the table of football players.

"Can you believe that?" Frank asked, shaking his head.

"And he actually asked us to go in with him!" Joe said in disbelief.

Chet sat up straight. "I'm doing it!"

Joe and Frank just stared at him. "What?" the Hardys said together.

"I'm going in with the Golden Boys!" Chet's round face looked determined. "I'm tired of being left to hang by myself. There's safety in numbers."

His expression turned bitter as he looked over at the table where Golden and his newly recruited crew were being rowdy.

"And the numbers are all around Terry Golden."

4 Getting Away with Murder

"You can't be serious!" Joe burst out as Chet started to get up from his seat. "Golden leans all over you, and you're going to try to go in with him?"

"Biff told me that's how you get into the Golden Boys. Everybody has to give you a rough time—at first." Chet shrugged. "It's sort of like an initiation."

"Oh, yeah?" Frank asked. "How about Dan Freeman? Is Golden initiating him, too?"

"That—that's different," Chet said. "He tangled with Terry."

"Only after Terry started it." Joe was about to argue some more until he saw the stubborn expression on Chet's face.

Instead Joe sank back in his seat, sighing. "I hope you know what you're getting into."

"I know what I'm getting out of." Leaving his tray, Chet walked over to Golden and his boys. Terry seemed to be in a good mood. After ribbing him a little, he sent Chet off to get him a soda. Chet seemed to be relieved as he went on the errand. He couldn't see the look Wendell Logan sent after him.

"Trouble," Joe said, shaking his head. "This is going to mean trouble."

Trouble was the last thing on Frank's mind as he fought the mob scene in the halls at dismissal. The school had just about cleared out by the time he strolled to his locker.

He was in no hurry today. His college course didn't meet on Thursdays, and he'd caught up on all his classwork. For once, Frank had a free afternoon. So, of course, Callie *wasn't* free.

"I made plans with Iola Morton to go to the library," Callie told him. "Both of us have projects we need to research. And since you're never around, I figured it would be all right."

Frank didn't want to spend his afternoon in the library, even to be with Callie. And most of his buddies—Joe, Chet, Biff Hooper—were on the football team.

I suppose I could hang out in the bleachers and

watch them practice. Frank shook that thought away. That would also mean watching Terry Golden.

Frank reran the scene from lunch in his head. He'd wanted to do something when Golden started in on Chet, but what? Fighting with Terry would land them both in the assistant principal's office.

Frank could just imagine the look on Mr. Sheldrake's face. "Chocolate cake? The two of you got into a fight over someone else's chocolate cake?"

So Frank had done nothing. The memory made him feel a little sick.

Guess feeling that way kills the idea of hanging out with Tony Prito at Mr. Pizza, he thought.

Frank was walking down the main hall of the oldest part of the school. The wall tiles had faded to an off-yellow color. The next turn would take him into the south wing, with its newer, shinier walls—where his locker was located.

He stopped before he came to the turn, though, cocking his head. What was that?

The muffled, thumping noise sounded again.

Curious, Frank leaned around the corner.

He stared in shock.

The sound came from Dan Freeman, clumping along on only one shoe. That wasn't all he was missing. Spindly legs poked out from under his shirttails like a pair of toothpicks.

Dan wasn't wearing pants!

"Freeman—Dan!" Frank's words stumbled over themselves in surprise. "What happened?"

"A couple of gorillas happened." Dan's usually pale face was bright red. "I got pantsed!"

He looked down at his bare legs. "How am I supposed to get home like this?"

"My locker is right here," Frank said. "Let's see what I've got."

Unfortunately, Frank's gym clothes were at home in the wash. He did offer his jacket to Dan, who tied it around his waist.

"That's a little better," Dan said.

"Did Terry Golden do this to you?" Frank asked.

"You were in English class," Dan replied bitterly. "What do you think?" He shook his head. "Actually, it was a couple of guys from his goon squad. That animal Logan, Biff Hooper . . ."

"They probably just tossed your pants somewhere," Frank interrupted. "Maybe we can find them before someone else does."

"Find what, Mr. Hardy?"

The voice came from around the corner, but Frank knew to whom it belonged. A second later Mr. Sheldrake came into view. Tall and pale, he was the assistant principal, in charge of school discipline. The kids called him Old Beady Eyes.

His eyes were pretty wide now as he took in Dan Freeman.

31

"I always take a quick look around the halls after school." Sheldrake shook his head. "You never know what you'll find."

He turned to Frank. "Mr. Hardy?"

"He was just trying to help me, sir," Dan said.

The assistant principal shook his head. "Why don't you come down to my office, Mr. Freeman? And, Mr. Hardy, maybe you can look for what your friend—er—lost."

The halls of the south wing were empty, and they echoed as Frank searched for Dan's pants. Most of the classroom doors were closed and locked. Frank found Dan's shoe halfway down the stairs at the end of the corridor. His pants were hooked on the handle of the swinging doors that opened into the stairwell.

Some sense of humor, Frank thought as he pulled them loose. He stopped, the image of Biff's laughing face rising up before him.

First he goes after Chet, now Dan . . . that wasn't like Biff at all.

Why can't Golden do his own dirty work? Frank thought, giving the chinos a gentle shake. The tinkle of keys and change came from the pockets. A quick pat showed the wallet was in place, too. Nothing had been taken—except for the hit to Dan Freeman's pride.

Frank frowned as he headed for Mr. Sheldrake's office. He could see two shadows through

the pebbled glass window in the office door.

"I just want to make sure I'm getting this straight," Mr. Sheldrake said. "You had your pants stolen right off you. But you didn't catch even one glimpse of who did it?"

Dan's voice came through the glass. "It was just a couple of big guys. They came at me from behind. Next thing I knew, I was facedown on the floor and feeling a draft."

Frank knocked on the door.

"Yes?" Old Beady Eyes's voice sounded sharper than usual.

"Frank Hardy," Frank replied.

"Just a moment." The assistant principal unlocked the door. Frank had to fight the smile that came to his lips. Dan Freeman was sitting behind Sheldrake's desk.

Well, Frank thought. That's one way to hide your knobby knees.

He held out the shoe in his left hand, the pants in his right hand. "I found these in a stairwell in the north wing."

Mr. Sheldrake reached to take them. "I'm glad you found them," he said. "Otherwise, I'd have to ask Coach Devlin for some sweatpants."

The assistant principal's back was to Dan Freeman. He didn't see Dan flinch at the mention of the football coach's name.

Sheldrake put the pants and shoes on his desk.

33

"Why don't we step out for a moment to give Mr. Freeman some privacy."

Frank stood in the hallway with Old Beady Eyes. "Mr. Freeman is an excellent student," the assistant principal said. "He has one of the best minds in this school. So why would he think I'd believe his story about a sudden attack of blindness?"

Frank took a deep breath. "Maybe what he saw isn't as important as what happened to him earlier today."

Sheldrake looked at Frank, his eyes narrowing and getting beadier. "And what exactly was that, Mr. Hardy?"

"Dan had an argument with Terry Golden," Frank said. "It got pretty intense. For a second I thought Golden might end up swinging at him."

The assistant principal coughed as if something had stuck in his throat. "Terence Golden?" Sheldrake finally said. "From the football team?"

Frank nodded.

Behind them, the office door opened. Dan stood fully dressed again. He handed over Frank's jacket. Frank noticed that the other boy's chinos showed way too much sock.

"Do you think I could head home now?" Dan asked.

"Just a moment, Mr. Freeman." Old Beady Eyes aimed his best glare at Dan. "I understand you and

34

another student had a . . . difference of opinion."

Dan glanced in surprise at Frank. Then he gave an uncomfortable shrug. "It happens sometimes during classes. I guess being on the debate team gives me bad habits."

"This was an argument with a boy from the football team." Sheldrake's lips twisted, as though he didn't like the taste of the words he was about to say. "Terry Golden."

Dan shrugged again. "We disagreed about some poetry that Mr. Weeks was discussing."

"Just a disagreement?" Sheldrake pressed. "It couldn't have had anything to do with the incident involving your trousers?"

"I didn't see Golden when I lost my pants," Dan said.

That's probably true, Frank realized. Golden would be smart enough to stay out of sight. The only people he can get into trouble are Logan and Biff.

"You're sure?" the assistant principal asked, but he didn't seem to be trying very hard to question Dan.

"I know what I saw—uh, didn't see," Dan Freeman replied.

"You must realize the problem," Sheldrake said. "Unless you can identify the perpetrators, there's not much I can do."

Dan nodded, barely seeming to listen.

"Then I suppose you can go, Mr. Freeman," Old Beady Eyes said. "You, too, Mr. Hardy."

The next morning Joe Hardy was behind the wheel of the van as the brothers headed for school. He smoothly pulled into a space in Bayport High's parking lot.

As he was turning off the ignition, a horn blared.

"Hey! Nerd!" an all-too-familiar voice yelled. "Park that junker on the street with the rest of the losers. *I* need that spot."

Joe and Frank stared in amazement. A senior boy backed away from the only other empty spot in the row, and Terry Golden swung his car into the space.

"I don't believe this!" Frank burst out. "What is it about that creep that he always gets everything he wants?"

Joe gave a sour laugh and nodded through the van's windshield. "There's your answer."

A huge billboard had gone up on the roof of the school just as it did every year at this time. Foot-high letters told the story:

BAYPORT VS. SENECA
The Fall Classic!
Come cheer our team on to victory!

The date at the bottom of the sign was about a week away.

"You think that's why Golden is getting away

36

with murder?" Frank's voice showed his disbelief. "Because of a football game?"

"For folks around here, it's *the* football game," Joe replied. "We may not be as fanatical as some of those towns in Texas. High-school football is like a religion out there. But anybody who grew up in Bayport knows who our biggest rival is."

Frank nodded in agreement. "Seneca Tech."

"They're already talking about it on television." Joe went into his impersonation of the local sportscaster. "Coming up: the county's annual gridiron classic!"

Joe continued, "The mayors of both towns have made their little joke bets. That was on the news, too. It's a bushel of Bayport oysters against Seneca's best apple pies."

"Sure," Frank admitted. "But I notice that even you're saying it's a joke."

Joe shook his head. "It's no laughing matter, though. We managed to beat Seneca Tech last year. But what about the three years before that? Seneca really cleaned up with us. A lot of people in town don't want to see that happen again. If Terry boy can give us a win, I guess he *is* golden."

Frank looked at his brother. "Somehow, I didn't expect to hear that from you."

"Don't get me wrong," Joe said. "The guy's a real slimeball." He sighed and rubbed his eyes. "But if he helps the team—"

"Are you sure Golden is really doing that?" Frank asked. "It's bad enough that Chet and Biff have joined his crew. Look at the rest of the Golden Boys. Wendell Logan was a borderline bully when I was quarterback. Has hanging with Terry Golden made him a better person?"

Joe remembered the snap of the towel as Logan whipped it at Chet. "No, it hasn't. But the others have always been stand-up guys, on and off the field."

"But they've been acting like Golden lately, hoping his success will rub off on them." Frank shook his head. "Too high a price to pay for a win."

"They'll pay it, though." Joe gave a harsh laugh. "I think they'd do just about anything to beat Seneca Tech."

They had no more time to talk. The school doors opened, and kids began pouring in. Silently Joe and Frank joined the crowd.

Joe's morning started with math class. Next came history and gym. Coach Devlin led the calisthenics, then he passed out basketballs and let the kids choose teams. By lunchtime Joe had forgotten Frank's depressing words.

He joined the flood of kids heading for the cafeteria. The stairway was packed, as usual, but all of a sudden Joe spotted an opening in the crowd. As he headed for it, he saw wide shoulders and long

blond hair in the opening. Terry Golden. Space seemed to open up magically around the star jock.

Of course, it didn't hurt that Wendell Logan and Biff Hooper were on either side of him.

As Joe passed, he realized Golden seemed to be waiting for someone. A second later, he saw who. Dan Freeman hesitated for a second when he saw the jock. Then he quickly started to go by.

Golden spun around, his raised elbow clipping Dan on the back of the head.

"Oh, sorry." Golden smirked as the other boy staggered. "I didn't notice you there, nerd boy."

The moving crowd swept Freeman away before he could say or do anything.

Laughing, Wendell Logan flung out an arm. His big, beefy elbow caught another kid right in the side of the head. Joe recognized the victim—Phil Cohen, his friend and the class brain.

Logan's unexpected attack had caught Phil right at the top of the stairway.

Phil looked half-dazed as he stumbled forward. His feet went out from under him, and he plunged facedown toward the steep metal steps.

5 Lucky Catch

Logan was still laughing as Phil sent the guy in front of him forward. That kid was lucky enough to grab the banister and skip down a couple of stairs without falling.

Phil couldn't stop himself, though. He was either going to slide down the stairs facefirst or get trampled by the thundering herd led by the Golden Boys.

Joe took advantage of the open space around Terry and launched himself right between Golden and Logan.

"Hey!" Terry yelled as Joe brushed him aside.

Joe paid no attention. He'd have only one chance—

His left arm stretched out to grab the back of

Phil's pants. As his fingers wrapped around Phil's leather belt, Joe swung his right hand out to catch the banister.

If I don't get it, we're both taking this flight of stairs the hard way, he thought.

Phil gave out a "whooof!" as Joe's hold yanked his belt tight against his stomach. Joe's right hand slipped on the banister, and he only managed to slow Phil, not stop him. Now they were both going down.

Joe tried to grab the railing again but missed. It was too late.

Just then a muscular arm clamped under Joe's armpit. "Hang on to Phil!" a voice grunted in his ear.

Joe found himself being hauled upright and fought to keep his grip on Phil.

Just when Joe felt as though his arm was going to pop off, Phil managed to grab hold of the banister and slow his descent. As Phil pulled himself upright, Joe turned to the guy who'd saved them both.

Biff Hooper.

"Man, am I glad you held on to Phil," Biff said.

"Wouldn't have worked without your backup," Joe said. "We both could have broken our necks—"

"Or at least wound up with footprints all over our backs." Now that he was safe, Phil could attempt a joke. "Thanks, Joe. And thanks, Biff."

No thanks to Golden and Logan, Joe thought. He peered over Phil's shoulder to Golden and Logan, farther down the stairs.

Whatever Terry Golden was thinking, he'd hidden it behind a poker face. Wendell Logan, however, had turned and was glaring up at them all. You'd think he'd just run a play for the opposing team, Joe thought.

Frank Hardy looked up as Joe and Phil brought their trays to his table in the cafeteria. Both guys appeared to be a little shaken. "What's up?" he asked.

"We were," Phil replied. "And then we were almost down."

As Frank listened to the story, he went from surprised to angry. "That was a really stupid thing for them to do. What's Old Beady Eyes going to do about it?"

Phil shook his head. "I'm not going to Sheldrake. Coach Devlin would just get them off."

"Not if I backed you up," Joe said.

"Yeah—great idea." Phil sighed and shook his head. "Then we can both be the guys who blew Bayport's chances in the Seneca game."

Frank watched as Joe's mouth snapped shut. His younger brother hadn't thought that far ahead.

"It's still not right," Joe finally said. "There must be something we can do."

"Not with me," Phil said.

"How about me?" Frank suggested. "Coach Devlin is probably in his office. We can eat quickly and pay him a visit."

"Unless it's another piece of paper, come in," Coach Devlin called when they knocked on his door. When he and Joe went inside, Frank understood the greeting. Every inch of the coach's desk was covered with piles of forms or reports.

Coach Devlin shifted some papers around. "This is the part of coaching that never makes it into sports movies," he said. "I wonder why."

He looked from Joe to Frank. "Can I hope that you've decided to leave the college courses until you're in college?"

Frank grinned, shaking his head. "You seem to be doing fine with Eddie Taplinger, Coach."

"I'd be happier if I had . . . more than one string to my bow."

Frank's grin got wider. Coach Devlin had almost said the words that no player wanted to hear "second string." But he'd gotten around it gracefully.

Joe got it, too. "It's the first string we're worried about," he said. "Wendell Logan almost sent a kid down a flight of stairs before lunch. He was following the lead of his pal Terry Golden, who'd used this move on another kid a few seconds before."

The coach rested his hands on two different

43

piles of paper. "Something that serious should be taken up with Assistant Principal Sheldrake. Why are you talking to me?"

"The kid who took the knock won't go to Mr. Sheldrake," Joe said. "He thinks you'd just get the players off. He also doesn't want to mess things up for the Seneca game."

Coach Devlin nodded. "And what's your interest, Frank?"

"I share a class with Terry Golden and the kid he clipped, Coach. There's bad blood between them."

"I see," the coach said. "And what would you like me to do? Kick him and Logan off the team? Suspend them? Forfeit the Seneca game?"

"What?" Joe said. "No! We thought—I thought . . . you'd tell them to cool it."

"Right now Terry Golden thinks he can get away with anything," Frank said. "That's what he told a teacher. I'm hoping he'll listen to you if you tell him otherwise."

"And this teacher had nothing to say to him?" asked the coach.

"Hey, if you don't believe us—" Joe began.

Coach Devlin shook his head. "I just want to make sure, that's all. There's been no official comment on any team member's conduct?"

"No," Frank admitted. "That's why we're here . . . unofficially."

44

The coach nodded. "Sometimes you have to do these things a little unofficially—for the sake of the team. For instance, you never made a stink after that shot Terry gave you at practice."

"You saw that?" Joe asked, astonished.

"And I didn't get all bent out of shape about it, either," Devlin said. "You know what it's like before a big game. There's always a certain amount of . . . horseplay."

"Logan was playing way too rough on the stairs," Joe protested. "Our friend Phil could have broken his neck."

"But he didn't," the coach said. "You asked me to tell the team to cool it. What if I do . . . and what if the team is too cool for the Seneca game?"

"I don't think—" Frank began.

"I don't think you or Joe or anybody would thank me for that," Devlin said. "I don't think anybody in this town would be happy about it."

Frank stared at his brother. Was the coach even hearing what they were saying?

"I appreciate that you boys came to me," Coach Devlin said. "Don't worry about it." He turned to Joe. "Especially you—I want you ready for the Seneca game, too."

Frank shook his head as he and Joe left the office. He felt as though he'd taken a quick trip through the Twilight Zone.

"I guess you're right, Joe," Frank said. "The only

thing anyone around here wants to hear about is beating Seneca."

Joe shrugged as they headed to class. "I can understand it a little more coming from the coach," he said. "His contract runs out this year. A win over Seneca would help him keep his job."

"So we'll put up with a little bullying and a few hazing games," Frank said angrily. "It's just a little horseplay. What will it take to get their attention? Someone getting killed?"

Frank was still fuming when classes were dismissed. He jumped when Callie poked him in the arm. "Earth to Frank. Are you giving me a lift today?"

"What? Sorry, Callie," he apologized.

"You were daydreaming all through class," she said. "Did you hear anything Patel had to say?"

Frank looked down at the empty pages of his notebook.

"Guess not," he confessed. "I hope you did a better job than I did."

"I tried," Callie said. "Maybe you can explain what I wrote down." She looked at Frank. "What's the matter? It's not that special class, is it?"

Frank shook his head. "Nah," he said, with a wry grin. "It's a case of people doing to me what I just did to Mr. Patel—paying no attention. Let's get out of here."

46

They got out into the parking lot just as the football team came trooping out of the gym exit. Most of the players hustled through the faculty parking lot on their way to the athletic field.

Frank noticed one car had its red parking lights on. It was the little subcompact model Mr. Weeks drove.

Frank spotted Terry Golden as he grabbed hold of Wendell Logan and Biff. He whispered to them, then went over to Mr. Weeks's car.

"Hold it, guys!" he shouted. "Mr. Weeks wants to get out."

The team members halted. Terry made a big production out of directing traffic while the teacher backed out of the space and pulled around.

By the time Mr. Weeks was ready to go, Golden was standing in front of the car with Biff and Logan on opposite sides of the rear bumper.

"I can't move with you standing there," Mr. Weeks said.

"Oh, gee, Mr. W.," Golden said. "We just want to give you a *lift!*"

That was the signal for the two linemen to pick up the back of the car. Terry jumped out of the way, and the rear wheels began to spin uselessly in midair.

"Those guys are crazy." Callie moved closer for a better look at the show.

Biff and Wendell were big, and the car was small—for a car. Even so, it was heavy. They lost their grip on the bumper, and the rear end of the car came down with a crash.

The wheels didn't set down together, though. And they were still moving. As soon as they hit the ground, the tires squealed. The car swerved wildly and shot forward . . .

Straight for Callie!

6 Discovery in the Dark

Frank had just one chance to keep Callie from becoming a smear on the pavement. He threw himself forward.

Callie still hadn't moved when Frank crashed into her and caught her around the waist. He yanked her off to the side.

A second later Mr. Weeks's car screeched through the space where they'd been.

The teacher finally managed to bring his vehicle to a stop. Pale-faced, he burst from behind the wheel. "Are you all right?" he asked Callie, who was still on the ground.

"Just a little shaken up," Callie answered, and waved the man on. Callie looked at Frank. "You

might be a quarterback, but you sure know how to tackle. Thanks."

Frank helped his girlfriend up, then he stalked over to Biff and Wendell Logan. "Hey—geniuses!" he snapped.

Biff at least looked embarrassed.

Logan tried to pass the blame. "Weeks was the one who gunned the engine."

"What a weird idea, considering he was in his car," Frank said sarcastically. "Of course, he wasn't expecting the human jacks here." He shook his head. "Do you do *everything* Golden tells you?"

"We're all on the same team, Hardy." Terry Golden stepped forward to thrust his face into Frank's. "But you wouldn't know about that anymore. You turned your back on the team."

"Yeah. I can see what I've been missing."

Letting out a long breath, Frank turned away and headed back to Callie. Getting into a fight with a would-be football hero was more trouble than it would be worth.

When the Saturday of the Seneca game came around, Frank wasn't even near the playing field. He had to spend the afternoon in the library. It was almost empty, so he got a lot of work done.

Even in the quiet building, he could hear the hooting and hollering in the streets outside. From the sound of it, Bayport High had won.

Later, back at the Hardy house, the celebration continued with friends of Frank and Joe's. Callie slipped an arm through Frank's as they watched Joe get his hand shaken and his back pounded.

Aunt Gertrude pointed at the clock. "Time for the evening news."

Must have been a quiet news day, Frank thought. The lead story was the Bayport victory over Seneca. Joe's smile slipped a little when he saw that all the game footage was of Terry Golden.

Then came the post-game interview and Terry Golden's grinning face. He raised a fist in the air and shook it. "Now we have something to celebrate!" he shouted from the television screen.

That piece of film also showed up on Sunday's news.

Frank got out of his computer class early on Monday. Instead of heading straight home, he drove over to Bayport High.

Football practice should be over just about now, Frank thought. I bet Joe would appreciate a lift home.

But as Frank drove up to the school he found himself steering away from the athletic field. He still was in no mood to deal with Terry Golden.

Instead, Frank parked at the main entrance of the school. He chuckled to himself as he noted that the front steps and flagpole looked naked

without the usual crowd of kids hanging out.

I can cut straight through the school and catch Joe at the locker room, Frank thought, pushing the door open. He stepped into an empty, echoing corridor with the yellowed tile walls. Once this had been the main hallway of the school. Now it was a little-used cross-corridor because most of the classrooms were in the newer wings.

All at once the hallway was neither empty nor quiet. A loud, braying laugh bounced off the tiled walls, quickly drowned out by heavy, clumping footfalls.

Frank recognized the big guy who came pounding round the corner as a linebacker on the football team. A second later another kid came running after him. The second kid wasn't small, but it would take two of him to equal the size and weight of the football player.

He had almost caught up when the linebacker swung around. He had a knapsack in each hand. One of the bags caught his pursuer in the stomach.

The smaller kid crumpled, the breath knocked out of him. His attacker kept running. Frank moved to block the guy, but he never got the chance. The linebacker turned before he reached the school exit. Instead, he banged open a door marked No Admittance.

Frank blinked in surprise. That wasn't a way out. The door guarded the stairs to the school

basement, an area that was off-limits to all students.

In the split second before the door shut, Frank saw something else. The football player had two other book bags hanging from his shoulders.

Frank went up to the kid who'd been chasing the linebacker. He looked vaguely familiar. Frank remembered a picture in the *Beacon*. This guy was one of the debate winners. John something? Or was it Jerry? No. Jimmy.

"Jimmy Brooks," Frank said, going down on one knee. "What happened?"

The kid pushed himself up off the floor, his face still twisted in pain. "They just burst in on our debate meeting, grabbed our books, and took off. I—I tried to follow—"

His hand went to his stomach as he remembered what happened.

"Okay, you've shown you have got guts," Frank told him. "Now show you've got brains. Come with me to Mr. Sheldrake."

Jimmy turned toward the basement door. "But our books—"

"Don't go down there alone," Frank said, helping the other boy to his feet. "Let Old Beady Eyes take care of it."

They had crossed the corridor, heading straight for the assistant principal's office when they heard footsteps come running their way. Jimmy's

shoulders hunched, bracing for another fight.

It was Joe Hardy, his hair standing up in spikes, and the front of his shirt buttoned wrong. He looked from Frank to Jimmy Brooks. "It's the Golden Boys," he said. "They're beating up kids to celebrate beating Seneca. And Chet's set up to be number one on their hit parade."

"Go on to Mr. Sheldrake," Frank told Jimmy, sending him down the hall. Then Frank turned to his brother. "What are they doing?"

"I'm not sure," Joe said. "When I got out of the showers, I overheard Wendell Logan talking to Biff. Logan said the Great Raid was on for today. 'Fatso Morton thinks he's in on it.' " Joe did a decent Logan impersonation. " 'He is—but on the receiving end.' "

Joe switched back to his own voice. "Biff got really upset. He was out of there before I could ask anything. And when Logan saw me, he got out, too."

"I saw part of what happened," Frank said. "They broke up a debate meeting—grabbed the guys' books. Jimmy Brooks was trying to follow Matt Walinovski and got nailed. Matt took off and went down there." He pointed to the basement stairwell.

"I don't like the sound of that," Joe said. "It's dark and quiet down there."

"You've been down in the basement?" Frank asked.

54

Joe shrugged. "Just to check it out. You know— find out why they didn't want anyone down there."

"Then you should know your way around." Frank headed for the door. "Lead on."

He noticed two things once they were past the forbidden entrance. The cinderblock walls hadn't been painted in a long time, and the lights were even dimmer than he expected. "Was it this dark when you were down here last?" Frank lowered his voice.

Joe shook his head. "Nuh-uh."

In the distance, they heard a popping sound, and the tinkle of glass. The light in the basement became even dimmer.

"Some clown is breaking light bulbs," Joe muttered.

A loud, boisterous voice yelled, "Yo, nerd!"

Then came what sounded like a slap, followed by a cry of pain.

"Didn't like that?" the loud voice taunted. "How about this?"

A sickening thud echoed from the darkness ahead of them. Frank realized his teeth were clenched tightly together. That sounded like someone being thrown into a wall.

The Hardys groped their way forward. The halls were narrow and snaked around odd-shaped rooms. The boys had to detour around piles of dusty supplies.

They reached a section where the overhead sockets still had bare, dim bulbs.

A human form lurched into view from a side hallway. The kid had started the day in a white shirt. Now it had filthy handprints all over it—not to mention drops of blood dribbling down from his chin.

The boy rubbed the back of a dusty hand across his face, smearing the bloody trickle. His wild eyes locked on them.

"Don't go in the dark parts!" the kid warned, his words slurred because of his split lip. "They're waiting in the dark parts!"

"Get out of here—now!" Frank ordered. "Get upstairs and tell Mr. Sheldrake. Move!"

He turned to his brother as they let the kid go by. Joe's face was grim, his hands clenched into fists.

"Nice games they're playing," he said. "Maybe we can even up the sides."

They turned down the corridor the victim had taken. The hall quickly became dark, but there was no one there. Whoever had roughed up the kid had taken off.

Frank ran his fingers along the wall as they moved forward. When they hit a lighted area again, he saw that his whole hand was grayish black. "Coal dust," he said, rubbing his fingers together. "We must be near the old boiler room."

"Speak of the devil." Joe pointed to a riveted iron door ahead of them and to the left. Faded red letters identified the URNAC   OOM.

"Furnace Room," Frank said, deciphering the partial lettering. "I guess they just left the old coal-burning furnace here when they switched to oil heat." Frank rubbed his hands together in another attempt to get them clean. "Too bad they didn't get rid of all this dust."

Joe, however, pointed to the door. "Looks like it was all locked up—once."

The door was old and rusty, but bright scratches showed in the metal where a padlock had been pried away.

They were about to turn away when they heard a scraping from the other side of the door. Frank looked at Joe. "Better check it out."

He put a palm against the cold metal and pushed. The door swung in with a rusty screech, and the light from the bulb over their heads invaded the darkness.

A figure sprang into being before them as if it had been hit by a spotlight . . . a chubby, blinking figure.

Chet Morton's right eye was swelling up in a definite shiner. He faced the Hardys with an old coal shovel raised up in both hands to defend himself.

Book bags and a bundle of old clothes lay at Chet's feet.

Frank drew his breath in sharply as he realized that it was no bundle on the floor.

It was a tall, muscular body with short-cropped, sandy hair—Biff Hooper.

And he lay there way, way too still. . . .

7 Big Trouble

"Chet, what did you do?" Joe burst out. He charged forward, kicking several book bags out of his way until he could drop to his knees beside Biff.

Chet, who had the shovel up shoulder height, ready to swing, stumbled backward, his shoulders sagging in relief as he recognized Joe's voice.

"Am I glad to see you guys!" Chet gasped.

Joe didn't answer. All his attention was on Biff. He extended one hand, gently feeling Biff's neck. "There's a pulse," he announced. "But it's weak— very weak!"

Chet was now looking down at Biff, his face a mask of horror. The shovel dropped from his hands to clatter on the floor. "Oh, no! Biff! What happened to him?"

Frank gave his friend a long look. "You don't know?"

Chet's eyes didn't leave Biff's still form. "It was supposed to be an initiation," he said tightly. "The guys had a prank planned."

His hand went to the bruise around his eye. "I thought I'd come in for a little trouble, but I didn't expect rough stuff. From the sounds, some kids were getting it worse than I was. I moved away . . . saw the boiler room, figured it would be a good place to hide."

"What about Biff?" Frank asked.

"I don't know!" Chet's voice rose. He looked terribly upset. "I was checking behind me to make sure nobody saw me going in here. You saw how dark it was. I took two steps and tripped—"

Chet gulped as he realized what he'd tripped over. "A-anyway, I groped around in the dark, and my hand found the shovel. I'd just gotten to my feet when you guys opened the door."

Joe popped up, grabbing Chet by the arm. "Chet, you've got to get out of here," he said. "I believe your story, but I don't know that everyone else will."

"It's too late, Joe." Frank pointed at the shovel. "Chet's fingerprints will be all over that. And the fact that it's so close to Biff—" He couldn't make himself say the words.

"That has to be what laid him out," Joe finished.

He dug in his pocket and got out some tissues. "So we'll wipe it clean—"

Frank reached out and pulled his brother back. "And what if you wipe away somebody else's fingerprints, too? You may be destroying the one thing that could clear Chet."

"So what do we do?" Joe asked in frustration.

"You're going upstairs to call an ambulance. And, like it or not, the cops."

"And you?" Joe asked.

"Chet and I are staying right here," Frank said. "To make sure the crime scene isn't disturbed."

"C-crime scene?" Chet stammered.

"You don't bang your head on a shovel accidentally. Biff's on the floor because somebody put him there," Frank said. "It's our job to help find out who did it."

Joe set off down the corridor at a run. Frank and Chet stood guard in the doorway. Every few minutes Frank stepped around the scattered book bags to check on Biff. He wasn't doing any worse. But he was still unconscious—and not getting any better.

"Think, Chet. Is there something, anything else you can remember? Did you see anybody on your way here?"

"I was kind of rattled after taking that pop in the eye," Chet said. "It was Wendell Logan, I think. The guy can punch!"

He frowned, trying to remember. "It was kind of like playing hide-and-seek. You didn't want people to see you. Any of the Golden Boys would give you a shot. They were herding us away from the stairs."

Chet shuddered. "I just tried to get through the lighted areas as quickly as possible. And in the dark, well, I was quiet and careful. Logan punched me out in the dark. I couldn't see his face, but I couldn't miss that laugh."

After a moment Chet shook his head. "That's all I remember."

They spent a little while in silence. Then flashlight beams cut the darkness in the distance. "You're sure this is the way?" a gruff voice asked.

"Straight ahead," Joe Hardy's voice replied.

A pair of cops and a couple of paramedics came into the lighted area.

"In here!" Frank called.

The medical people immediately went to work getting Biff on a stretcher. The lead police officer looked from Biff to the shovel on the floor and then to Chet's eye. "I guess you boys will have some questions to answer," he said.

The look he gave them was not friendly and definitely suspicious when it fell on Chet.

Joe and Frank were late for supper. Their father had picked them up from police headquarters when the questioning was over. Fenton

Hardy's face was grim as he steered the car for home.

"It doesn't look good for Chet," he said after hearing what the boys had to say.

"I figured that from the looks the cops were giving him," Joe said.

"I started out as a cop, too," Fenton reminded them. "And if we found someone standing over a victim holding a shovel. Well, that pretty much made the case."

"This is Chet we're talking about," Frank said. "Do you really think he'd whack Biff like that?"

"Chet has a weightlifter's build," Fenton replied. "There's plenty of muscle on his frame."

"I'm not asking whether it's physically possible," Frank objected. "Chet's not—"

"In the dark, with people chasing him, Chet might have swung first and asked questions later," Fenton said.

Joe was ready to back up Frank's arguments when he remembered his own first reaction to seeing Biff.

I asked Chet why he'd done it, he thought, shutting his mouth.

"If Chet had swung on anyone, I think he would have told us." Frank glanced at Joe. "I can't imagine he was in any shape to try covering things up."

The boys arrived home, and Aunt Gertrude began serving supper. When she and Mrs. Hardy

heard the story, they quickly came in on Chet's side.

"I can't believe you're saying that boy is guilty!" Aunt Gertrude turned accusing eyes on Fenton.

"I didn't say he was guilty," Fenton protested. "The situation does seem stacked against him, though."

"I'll take care of the boys," Laura Hardy told Aunt Gertrude. "I know your program is coming on."

Aunt Gertrude was a loyal viewer of the ten o'clock news. The sportscaster had a contest going, and she was convinced she was going to win.

Mrs. Hardy turned to her husband. "Is it really as bad for Chet as you're saying?" she asked quietly.

Fenton shook his head. "Hard to see how it could get worse."

Aunt Gertrude's voice suddenly erupted from the living room. "Everyone! In here!"

When Joe, Frank, and their parents rushed in, they found Aunt Gertrude pointing at the TV screen. Behind the BayNews anchorperson floated the words "School Attack."

The anchor, a young blond woman, frowned as she gave the report. "Reports are still sketchy. Several members of Bayport High's football team, victors in Saturday's game against Seneca Tech, found themselves in a violent incident—"

" 'Found themselves'?" Joe echoed. "They started it!"

"Lineman Allen 'Biff' Hooper was admitted to Bayport General Hospital in a comatose condition. A teammate was found with him—"

The screen then switched to a picture of Chet Morton.

Fenton shook his head. "I was wrong. It could get worse for Chet."

The newswoman continued her report and finished with, "BayNews reporters contacted several members of the school board. But none had any comment on how such an attack could have occured."

"She made Golden and his gang sound like victims," Joe said in disbelief.

"For now they're still football heroes," Fenton pointed out. "If that changes—"

He was interrupted by the doorbell.

"Now, who could that be at this time of night?" Aunt Gertrude switched off the set and went to answer the door.

She came into the room a moment later with Mr. and Mrs. Morton, Chet's mom and dad.

"I'm terribly sorry—" Laura Hardy began.

Mr. Morton interrupted her. "What we need is help."

Joe sometimes kidded Chet that his friend was seeing his future when he looked at his father. Mr. Morton had the same stocky frame as Chet . . . but a much bigger stomach. He'd lost almost all the

hair on the top of his head except for a little tuft just over his forehead. He was a successful businessman, but something in his appearance made people want to smile.

Seeing him in a blue velour jogging—or rather, lounging—suit should have been funny. Knowing that he'd probably rushed from his home to help his son made it no laughing matter. "We've been down with the police since they called us. I don't care what it costs, I want you to find out what really happened in that basement, Fenton."

"Who do you have handling Chet's case?" Fenton asked.

"Lew Cadwalader. He takes care of all our real estate—"

"I'm sure he's a good real estate lawyer," Fenton said, "but I'd recommend Charlie Sponato for this. Let me write down his number."

Mr. Morton frowned as Fenton handed him the piece of paper. "What does this Sponato do?"

"He's a criminal attorney," Fenton said. "You'll find he's more familiar with the system—"

"I don't care about the system!" Mrs. Morton burst out. "I just want my son out of jail!"

Gazing at Mrs. Morton, Joe could see where her daughter, Iola, got her good looks. But Mrs. Morton seemed to have aged ten years since the last time Joe had seen her.

"I'm afraid you have to understand the system

so you'll know what you're up against." Fenton's voice was gentle but firm. "The police didn't just pick Chet's name out of a hat. They look for things like motive, opportunity, and means."

He glanced over at Frank and Joe. "From what my sons tell me, several boys on the football team—including Biff—had been hazing Chet."

Mr. Morton's broad face took on a reddish tinge. "Why am I hearing about this now? Why didn't the school do something?"

"They were hurting Chet?" Mrs. Morton asked in shock.

"Teasing him, mainly," Frank said.

"Snapping towels—stuff like that," Joe added.

"Things he wouldn't have reported unless he wanted to look like a crybaby," Fenton said grimly. "The teasings do give the police—and the prosecutor—a motive."

He held up two fingers. "Opportunity. Chet was down in the school basement because he thought he was taking part in a prank. It turned out to be a nasty attack on several boys . . . including your son. But he was definitely there."

Fenton took a deep breath. "As for means, Biff suffered a severe blow to the head, probably from a shovel found at the scene." He hesitated. "Chet was holding that shovel."

Mrs. Morton choked back tears.

Mr. Morton put his arms around his wife and

glared at Fenton. "Why are you telling us all these upsetting things?"

"As I said earlier, you have to understand what you're up against. The police have to know everything I said now in order to hold Chet."

"Motive, opportunity . . . means. That's what they use to convict"—Mrs. Morton's voice faltered—"m-murderers."

Fenton shook his head unhappily, but tried to reassure Mrs. Morton. "Biff's going to pull through; he's a strong kid."

Chet's mother was beyond consoling and burst into wild tears, clinging to her husband.

"I think that right now a good attorney might be your best help," Fenton said. "There's a strong case for self-defense—"

"You're saying Chet did what the police have accused him of!" Mrs. Morton said in a shrill voice.

"No, I'm not. He's caught in the system that's accused him," Fenton replied. "You want me—and the few people I employ—to do the job of a whole police department. I can't even guarantee we'd find anything. The best we might be able to do is spread out the suspicion point fingers in other directions. But you need a good lawyer—someone used to working in the system."

"What? Someone who can make a plea bargain?" Mr. Morton shook his head, his expression fierce. "My son told me he didn't hit that boy, and

I believe him. If someone doesn't believe he's innocent, I don't need them!"

He turned to his wife, gently leading her outside. It was as if a wall of ice had grown between the Hardys and the Mortons.

A piece of paper fluttered to the floor as the door slammed shut.

Joe picked it up. It was the number of the lawyer Mr. Hardy had written down for Mr. Morton.

8 Fact Finding

The Hardy family stood in silence . . . for about two seconds.

"I can't believe you did that," Laura Hardy said to her husband.

"Chet didn't put Biff in the hospital!" Joe insisted.

"I didn't say he did." Joe knew when his dad began talking in that tone of voice, his patience was just about running out. "I was suggesting that right now Chet needs a good lawyer more than he needs a detective. Like some other people, they were too emotional to hear me."

Laura Hardy gave her husband a level look. "What a surprise, considering the other upsetting things you were telling them."

"Things their lawyer apparently never told

them—or didn't succeed in getting through." Fenton snorted. "Not surprising, if he specializes in real estate."

Joe nodded. Dad had a point there.

"I just wanted Chet and Jill to understand that real life isn't like the lawyer shows on TV. People aren't usually saved by a big speech or a lucky clue popping up five minutes before the show ends. I spent too many years as a cop not to know how it really works."

Laura Hardy continued to glare at her husband. "And you couldn't break that to them more gently?" she asked. "Or was it Mr. Morton throwing his—ahem—weight around?"

"Like lawyers, private eyes usually have to deal with people who are in trouble—sometimes even hysterical," Fenton said.

"Like our friends the Mortons," Laura Hardy said.

Fenton nodded. "They're the worst kind of clients until they calm down a little. And I did give them the best advice I could. If they want to help Chet, they'd be better off looking for a good lawyer before they start looking at detectives."

"That doesn't mean that we can't start digging right away. Right, Dad? What do you say, Frank?" Joe questioned.

Frank nodded, and Fenton Hardy gave his approval. "You boys have a better idea of the sys-

tem, and you know what's happening at school. If Chet's parents couldn't get him out, even with a lawyer, that means Chet isn't *just* being questioned. He's been formally charged by the district attorney."

Frank frowned. "And if Biff takes a turn for the worse—"

Fenton nodded. "So will the charges."

The next morning, Tuesday, the boys left the house early, before school. Joe was behind the wheel, bringing the van downtown. He managed to find a parking space only a block from police headquarters.

"You think Con Riley will tell us anything?" Joe asked Frank as they got out of the van.

The older Hardy brother shook his head. "Probably not, if he's at his desk. But if we can catch him alone—there's a chance!"

Officer Con Riley was just coming out the door of the building, and Joe and Frank rushed to catch up with him.

"How's it going, Con?" Joe asked. Both brothers were on a first-name basis with the big officer. He was the closest thing they had to a connection on the force.

"It will go a lot better after I have a shower, a shave, and some time in bed," Riley replied. His uniform was rumpled, and he was whiskery and red eyed.

"You look like you pulled an all-nighter," Frank said.

The police officer nodded. "With your friend Chet."

"If you're looking for a confession, I'd say you were out of line," Joe said.

"I'll tell you who was out of line," Riley said angrily. "Those television people! They should know better than to splash a kid's picture around like that."

Frank shrugged. "At least the TV people aren't holding an innocent kid in jail."

"Sticking up for your friend does you credit." Riley stretched and sighed. "And after spending a night talking to him, I have to say he's stuck to his story. But his prints are the only ones on that shovel—"

"That wasn't on the news," Joe said.

"And it won't be." Riley shook his head. "I must be half-asleep to give that away. I'll have to trust you boys to keep it quiet."

"Don't worry, Con," Joe said.

No way would they be spreading that fact around. It just made Chet look guiltier.

When Frank reached his homeroom that morning, he found a message waiting for him. "Mr. Sheldrake wants to see you right away."

Just as he reached the assistant principal's

73

office, who came walking down the hall to join him? Joe Hardy.

"I guess we should have expected this," Frank said, opening the door.

Old Beady Eyes sat behind his desk and gestured to two empty chairs. "I'm hoping you'll be able to shed a little light on yesterday's . . . incident. According to Jimmy Brooks, you sent him to my office to report what was going on with the book bags. I'd like to hear exactly what happened after that."

Is it my imagination? Frank thought. Or is he nervous?

Shrugging, Frank started off with what he had seen in the hall. Joe added what he had overheard in the locker room, then they both told what happened after they met.

Sheldrake frowned, balancing a ballpoint pen between two fingers. He looked at Frank. "So, you can identify one of the football players involved." Then he turned to Joe. "And according to you, Mr. Logan and Mr. Hooper were also involved."

"Chet said Logan is the one who punched him," Joe said. "Isn't that what he told you, Frank?"

The assistant principal shook his head, looking definitely harassed. "I only want what *you* saw or heard," he said. "Not what other people told you."

"You make it sound like we'll be testifying in court," Frank said.

The assistant principal said nothing. But the uneasy look in his eyes got stronger.

Finally Sheldrake sighed. "You can go to class."

As the boys left the office, Joe turned to Frank. "What was that all about?"

"Information," Frank said quietly. "Last night the cops whisked us off to make a statement. Almost everything Sheldrake knows about this mess comes from what he heard on TV."

Joe's face lit with understanding. "And he's supposed to know everything that's going on in this school."

Frank nodded. "You can bet there'll be a lot of people worried about their jobs after this."

"As if it wouldn't be hard enough getting to the truth," Joe growled.

In English class Mr. Weeks didn't even try to control the students. "I hope you have as much fun with my replacement," he said.

For the first time, the class grew quiet. "Replacement?" Dan Freeman echoed.

I'll bet it hurts him to talk, Frank thought. Half of Dan's mouth was bruised and swollen.

Weeks nodded. "I am—I was—the moderator for the debate team. That mean's I'm responsible for not stopping what happened yesterday."

The teacher suddenly looked very young. "I don't see any reason to drag things out, so I

75

offered my resignation this morning. As soon as the school board chooses a replacement, I'll be out of here."

"But—but—" Dan sputtered.

"No more to discuss," Weeks said grimly. "Let's move on to a few dusty old sonnets."

Frank waited behind after the classroom emptied for lunch. Mr. Weeks was slowly packing up his materials. "Yes, Mr. Hardy?"

"I'll be sorry to see you go," Frank said.

The teacher shook his head. "One thing this school has taught me—I'm no great loss."

"What will you do?"

"Go back to school again, maybe," Weeks said. "See if I can be a teaching assistant for an older set of students."

"You seem to be taking what happened yesterday pretty hard."

Weeks stared at the floor. "A student almost died because I froze. I sat there like a lump when those four yahoos came in and stole the debaters' books. When I finally moved, I couldn't get the door open. One of them was holding it closed. I lost control of the students—some of the boys went after the bullies."

He sighed. "And then I panicked, chasing after them. If I'd gone immediately to Mr. Sheldrake—"

The young teacher bit his words off. "But I

76

didn't. And as a result, young Mr. Hooper is in the hospital."

Weeks managed the ghost of a smile. "Mr. Sheldrake considers me totally useless. I didn't recognize any of the boys who grabbed the books."

"None of them were in your classes?" Frank asked. "I thought you might have seen Biff or Wendell Logan. I'm sure you'd remember them, after the stunt they pulled with your car."

The teacher shook his head. "No. I didn't recognize any of the boys I saw. And as you say, I'd have good reason to remember the pair who held up my car." He shook his head. "That incident alone should have convinced me to look for another line of work."

Weeks headed for the door, and Frank followed, deep in thought. A certain amount of planning had gone into the operation of the day before. Grabbing the book bags to lure the nerds to the basement. Using kids who wouldn't be recognized to carry out the dangerous bits . . .

Sure. Terry Golden would have been picked out in no time. He was probably the one who'd targeted the debate team. Chet thought he was in on an initiation prank, so he was down in the basement. But he had recognized Wendell Logan's laugh while getting punched down there. It looked as though Biff hadn't even been involved, although he must have had some idea of what was going to

happen. Certainly, he knew where to go. That makes at least four people who were aware of the plan. . . .

Plus the four guys who actually grabbed the books. And then add in the victims. The school basement must have been pretty crowded.

Having made a start by putting faces on the bullies, Frank decided to try to identify the other side.

He headed down to the cafeteria. Most of the kids had finished eating lunch and were going outside. Frank caught Dan Freeman just as he was moving out the door.

"Looks like someone really hung one on you," Frank said.

"More than one." Dan's lips tightened when he turned and realized he was talking to Frank. Then he winced in pain.

Dan's voice was nasty when he spoke again. "I saw you hanging around after class to speak to Mr. Weeks. So, are you and your brother going to clear up the big mystery?"

He jammed his hands in his pockets. "Except it doesn't look like much of a mystery. Just another case of jocks versus nerds. This time, though, one of the jocks took things a little too far. He wound up taking out one of his own guys. Typical genius maneuver."

Frank had hoped to work a few questions into a casual conversation. Kiss that plan goodbye, he

thought. Dan read me like a book. And from the way he's talking, he wants to cut off any conversation before it starts.

"I don't think Chet hit Biff," Frank said to Dan's back as he started to walk away.

The other boy turned around. "Whoop-de-doo. I don't care, Hardy. Since yesterday, I've had more people than I can count asking me questions about this nonsense. They want names of kids who might have gone downstairs to the basement. They want me to ID the goons who were waiting for us. Did I see Hooper? Did I see Morton?"

Dan's bruised lips were set in an ugly line. "And you know what? I didn't tell them anything. *Nada.*"

Frank stared, a little surprised. "Don't you want—"

"I want to get out of this school and start my real life," Dan Freeman cut him off. "I want to put this whole thing behind me. So don't expect me to play detective games with you."

The bruised boy began stalking off, but he turned for one last word. "You want to help out your old teammate? Fine. Good for you."

Freeman jabbed a thumb at his own chest. "Just don't expect *me* to get all teary eyed because some muscle-headed jock got what he deserved."

9 Hits and Misses

Frank was surprised at the spurt of anger that shot through him. "And here I thought you were a smart guy, Freeman," he said sarcastically.

Dan Freeman glared back at Frank. "What's the problem? I don't have enough school spirit?"

"You don't have your facts straight," Frank told him. "Bad debating technique."

Dan had easily shrugged off taunts from Terry Golden, but Frank's words made him shake with rage.

Good thing he hasn't got a shovel handy, Frank thought.

"What *facts?*" Freeman made it sound like a dirty word.

"For one thing, Biff wasn't one of the guys who grabbed the bags," Frank said.

"There were more guys than—" Dan abruptly bit off his words. "Nice try, Hardy."

"That wasn't a try, that was a fact. Here's another. My brother was in the locker room when Biff heard this whole thing going down. Biff got pretty upset."

"Upset over missing out on all the fun?" Dan shot back. "He rushed right down when he heard about it."

"That's not what my third fact shows," Frank replied. "And this I saw with my own eyes."

"What's that?" Dan mocked.

"I saw Biff lying on the furnace-room floor," Frank said quietly. "And all around him, there were book bags." Frank took a step forward until he was right in Dan Freeman's face. "Biff was trying to get those books—and their owners—out of the basement."

For a second Frank managed to change Dan's bad attitude. Dan went pale and then stepped back.

But like any good debater, Freeman quickly rallied. "Brilliant deduction," he sneered. "I figure you just made your job twice as hard."

Frank frowned. "What do you mean?"

"If what you say is true, then Biff was trying to ruin the punching party his pals had set up. Maybe one of the jocks—like Chet—put a stop to that by putting a stop to Biff."

Dan's swollen lips twitched in a half-smile as he watched Frank's expression.

"Didn't think of that, did you?" the tall boy asked. "Maybe you should track down Terry Golden and try a couple of questions on him. A shovel to the back of the head sounds like his style."

Dan turned and started walking away again. This time Frank didn't try to stop him.

When Freeman stopped to glance back this time, he said, "Of course, if you try what I said, you may have to watch *your* back."

Frank was watching Dan Freeman walk off when a hand landed on his shoulder.

"Hey, bro," Joe Hardy said. "Where were you? I wound up having lunch with your girlfriend."

"Who just happens to have a little information," Callie Shaw said, stepping up beside them.

She dug in her shoulder bag and gave Frank a piece of paper. "Here are all the debate group guys who went out after their books."

Frank stared at the list of names. "How did you—"

"I got it from the *girls* on the debate team." Callie gave him a smug smile. "When those big bozos came in, they took *everybody's* books. The stuff belonging to the girls was left piled in the hall. The creeps were definitely after the boys. I guess they

figured that after taking the trouncing they had planned, the boys would be too humiliated to talk about it."

"It might have gone that way, too," Joe said. "Get the nerds down in the dark, work them over hard and quick, and get out of there. All the debate kids would have was a bunch of bruises and nobody they could point a finger at."

Frank nodded. "But then the plan went off the track."

"You mean *we* turned up?" Joe said.

"*Biff* turned up and began helping the debate guys."

"And somebody hit him for that—hard." Callie suddenly looked a little sick.

Frank held up his piece of paper. "According to this, seven debate guys left the classroom in pursuit of their books. One of them was Jimmy Brooks."

"That's the guy you sent to Mr. Sheldrake," Joe said.

"And we know he went, because Old Beady Eyes mentioned him this morning," Frank went on. "So he wasn't down there in the dark. That leaves six debaters, including Dan Freeman."

"Mr. Coordination," Joe joked.

Frank ignored him. "From the football team, we've got the guy I saw in the hall—Walinovski. Then Chet, of course—"

"And Lousy Logan, who punched Chet out," Joe added. "There were three other guys who snatched the books."

"Plus the brains of the outfit—Terry Golden," Frank said. "He'd certainly be downstairs, waiting for a piece of Dan Freeman."

"So, besides Chet and Biff, there could have been a dozen people wandering around down there," Callie said.

"At least," Frank agreed. "And any of them could be responsible for what happened to Biff. The debate guys who were being terrorized would certainly see Biff as the enemy."

"But Biff's teammates—" Joe began.

"Might have seen him as the spoiler, stopping their little game," Frank finished. "Dan Freeman thought that bit with the shovel would be right up Terry Golden's alley."

From the look on Joe's face, he was struggling with the idea. "Golden, maybe," he said slowly. "But I'd hate to think that any of the other guys—"

He stopped, suddenly grim. "I guess I'll just have to ask some more questions."

"Just be careful." Callie shuddered. "It's bad enough having Biff in the hospital. Don't be his roommate."

The locker room was surprisingly quiet that afternoon. Usually the guys on the football team

kidded around as they changed into practice clothes. Today, though, there were no jokes. Teammates hardly spoke.

It was as though they were afraid, Joe thought.

Before sending them out to the field, Coach Devlin said he had a few words. "No doubt many of you are thinking about our two absent teammates today. I know we all hope for Biff to recover."

All the guys silently nodded.

"As for Chet, he's obviously facing a very difficult time. I hope he can prove his innocence. No one can be certain what went on yesterday evening."

The coach took a deep breath. "But I'm certain of this. In the name of team spirit, I tolerated a certain amount of . . . horseplay." He looked straight at Joe. "I didn't listen when people warned me that it might go too far. Consider this your first and only warning. From here on, there will be zero tolerance for any funny business. Try it—and you *will* regret it."

Devlin pointed to the door. " 'Nuff said. Let's move it!"

The guys got out of the locker room as if monsters were chasing them.

Practice that day was as rough as any Joe could remember. He stood wiping sweat off his forehead as Matt Walinovski staggered back from the tackling sleds.

"Coach is really running us ragged today," Joe said.

"Tell me about it!" Walinovski groaned. "I feel like somebody dropped a two-ton weight on me."

"A lot less heavy than those books you were toting yesterday."

Matt looked as if he'd just found himself on the wrong side of a tackle.

"You were seen, you know." Joe glanced over at the bigger guys on the team. "I was wondering who else was with you. Engels? Parisi? Logan would have been good for holding the door closed, but he was downstairs waiting for the fresh meat."

The other boy didn't say a word. But Joe noticed the way Walinovski reacted when his two buddies were named.

That gives us three out of four, he thought. The question is, how many others were in on this?

He tried talking to a few other guys. Most of them were worried about what people would think of the team, very few wanted to talk about what had happened. Nobody had anything to say when Joe wondered who was where—and when.

Eddie Taplinger walked over to him. "Don't look now," he said. "But there are TV cameras setting up over by the fence."

Joe glanced over to see Coach Devlin arguing with a news reporter.

"I don't think the coach is going to get any-

where," he said. "They have a right to be there. Freedom of information and all that."

"There's some information that never comes free," Eddie said. "And that includes the information you're digging for," the quarterback continued. "Golden spent last night making the rounds. He said there'd be a lot of people asking questions, and he told us to say nothing—stonewall them."

"For the good of the team," Joe said sarcastically.

"Better than hurting the team," Eddie retorted.

"Hey, I'm not some outsider poking his nose in. I'm trying to help Chet—he's a teammate, too."

"Golden said we should stonewall *everyone* who asks questions—especially you and your brother."

Joe gave a harsh laugh. "Then you may be looking for trouble, standing here talking with me."

Eddie nodded. "Maybe," he said. "But I figure somebody had to give you the heads-up."

A very angry Coach Devlin came back from the fence. The TV cameras remained in place, and the team sweated even harder for the rest of the practice session.

Joe was out of the showers and getting dressed when Wendell Logan loomed up beside him.

Looks like somebody told Golden about my questions, Joe thought. So he sent his pet over to scare me.

He ignored the bigger boy until Logan was almost touching him, his sweaty body sending off heat like a furnace. "I hear you're sticking your nose in where it isn't wanted," the big linebacker said.

"I certainly don't want to smell *you*," Joe replied. "So why don't you back off, Logan?"

"*You're* the one who'd better back off." Logan poked a big, meaty finger into Joe's chest. "Or you won't like what'll happen."

Joe decided to rattle Logan's cage a little. Maybe the big guy would let something slip. "What will you do?" he asked. "Punch me out, like you did Chet Morton? I guess it's a lot easier when you jump somebody in the dark."

Logan's big jaw dropped in shock. "How did—I mean—" His eyes moved to someone behind Joe. Then he scowled. "You got a mouth on you like that Freeman kid. Remember what happened to him."

"Yeah," Joe said. "He met someone else who was brave in the dark. You think you can hide until this all blows over, but too many people know bits and pieces of it. It will all come out, and everyone will know exactly what happened down in the basement."

Again Logan's eyes darted behind Joe for a cue. Joe stepped to one side, and turned to see who was behind him.

He saw Terry Golden slowly draw a finger across his throat.

Joe knew what that might mean. He quickly whipped around to face Wendell again.

But Logan was already taking a wild roundhouse swing.

A fist the size of a holiday ham was already flying at Joe's head!

10 Penalty Plays

Frank Hardy yawned, leaning back in his chair. His computer class didn't meet that day.

That didn't mean he had the afternoon off, though. Frank and the kids in the class were studying a new programming language, and Frank was still trying to get a simple program running in it.

He frowned, his fingers flashing over his computer keyboard. Maybe that particular order didn't belong there. . . .

When he tried to run the program again, the stupid thing still didn't work. Frank tried running the automatic debugger and wound up with a screen full of suggestions.

After reading what the computer had to say, Frank glanced at his watch.

Okay, he thought. One more round of debugging, then I've got to go to the library to pick up Callie.

Frank stared out at the growing late-afternoon shadows. After that, I guess we could catch Joe after practice. He made a face. See if his luck with the jocks was better than mine with the nerds.

Frank had spent the afternoon tracking down the names on Callie's list. Nobody wanted to talk about the incident. After coming home, he'd even tried calling a couple of the guys.

Unconsciously, Frank brought a hand to his ear. Nothing says "no comment" like having a phone slammed down, he thought. He turned back to the computer, determined not to think about it anymore.

Frank finally got to the point where at least he could start the program. Good enough, he decided, saving his work. He still had a couple of minutes to spare, so he checked his email.

He figured that the Bayport High grapevine had gotten the message that Frank Hardy was looking for information. Someone might decide to pass something along anonymously.

Sure enough, there was a message with an unfamiliar return address. Frank moved the arrow across his screen and clicked on the message.

The message was short, and not very sweet:

"Keep asking questions about what happened to Biff Hooper, and you'll be digging your own grave."

How nice, Frank thought. A threat. Let's see if we can backtrack and find out who sent it.

He tried to close down the message, but the computer didn't respond. Instead, patches began to appear on the screen. It was as if somebody inside the computer monitor were throwing dirt at the screen.

Oh, great. Frank had heard about this. It was the Gravedigger virus.

Must be a new version. It's obviously gotten past my antivirus defenses. He hesitated for a moment, then turned the computer off.

Better to crash the system than have it completely wipe out, he thought.

He looked at his watch again. Getting the computer back up again would be no problem. He'd made a recovery disk. But he'd have to go on to his dad's machine and download the latest software cure for the Gravedigger virus. That would take too long right now.

I don't want a dead computer *and* an annoyed girlfriend, he thought. He got up and headed downstairs for the van.

Callie was waiting for him outside the library. "How's it going?" she asked.

"I've had better days," Frank admitted. "Tried to

talk to a couple of the guys on your list, and they all ran away."

Callie grinned. "Could it be your breath?"

"You should see—or smell—the other guys," Frank said. "Some of them forget to brush their teeth." He went on to tell about the telephone hang-ups, then described the message on his computer.

"At least you managed to stir up something," Callie said.

"Yeah," Frank replied dryly. "Trouble. Opening that message let the Gravedigger virus into my computer."

"Oh, no!" Callie said. "Did it mess up everything on your hard drive?" She paused for a second. "Did it get to the stuff for your computer course?"

Frank winced. He hadn't thought of that. "Well, it will certainly give me something to talk about tomorrow. I just shut the computer down and came to get you." He gave her a smile. "We'll worry about the machinery later."

Pulling into the Bayport High lot to get Joe, Frank steered straight for the faculty parking area. "The lot's just about empty," he said. "And it's close to the gym entrance. I think I'll chance parking here."

Callie decided to stay in the van. "Sweat and liniment isn't my favorite perfume," she said.

Frank started to get out. Overhead, he noticed

that the sign for the Seneca game was being taken down.

"*Sic transit gloria mundi,*" he murmured.

"What?" Callie said.

"It's Latin—about the glories of the world passing away." He pointed at the sign. "The Seneca game was the biggest thing in town a week ago. Now it's history."

He went inside and walked along the side of the gym to reach the locker room. Frank started to push in the door . . . and paused.

It was quiet in there. *Too* quiet, as the old-time cowboy heroes would say. Usually, the guys would be cracking jokes or talking about practice.

Frank heard nothing at first. Then all at once he heard a grunt, followed by a metallic crash.

He pushed the door open quickly and stepped inside. The guys on the football team, most of them half-dressed, stood staring at Joe Hardy's locker.

Joe had one of Wendell Logan's arms twisted in a painful hold. The rest of the big linebacker seemed to be jammed into Joe's locker.

"What's going on out there?" Coach Devlin's voice came from his office. Joe dropped Logan's arm as the coach came around the lockers.

"See, Wendell," Joe said. "I said you'd never be able to fit in there."

The coach's expression was dubious as Logan

shakily extracted himself from the locker. He didn't say anything, though.

Joe looked over at Frank. "Oh, and here's my ride."

He quickly tossed his stuff into his gym bag. "See you, guys. Wendell . . . Terry."

Frank held the door as Joe breezed out.

Joe turned to his older brother with a grin. "You know that move you taught me? The one where you catch the guy's wrist when he throws a punch and use that to twist his arm?"

Frank nodded. He'd practiced that martial-arts move many times.

"Well, it worked. And it looks really impressive when the guy is much bigger than you are."

"I especially liked the touch where you got Wendell to play Sardines in your locker," Frank said. "I guess he was trying to discourage you from asking any questions?"

"More likely, Terry Golden was behind the discouraging." Joe suddenly smiled. "He doesn't know me very well, does he?"

"Did you get anywhere with your questions?" Frank asked.

Joe's smile slipped. "I managed to shake Walinovski up a little. Parisi and Engels may be involved. Other than that—" He shook his head. "Eddie Taplinger warned me. Ask questions, and the team will stonewall."

"Pretty much like Dan Freeman and his bunch." Frank growled in frustration. "We need something to pry a few stones out of these walls of silence."

"At least the debate team hasn't taken a swing at you," Joe pointed out.

"No, but I've got a hard drive on the critical list back home." Frank told Joe about the emailed threat and what happened afterward.

"Grave digging, huh?" Joe grinned, trying a joke. "Pretty messy business, when you come right down to it. You're not hip deep in dirt, you're six feet under."

Frank laughed as they walked through the gym. "Yeah, it's a business where you get in *under* the ground floor."

"I can dig it," Joe said, trying to top his brother.

Frank stopped abruptly, halfway through the gym. "With a shovel . . ." he said in an odd voice.

Joe looked a little concerned. "You feeling all right, Frank?"

Then he smacked himself on the forehead. "I guess that was kind of tasteless, considering how Biff wound up in the hospital."

Frank shook his head. "Think back to the moment we found Chet and Biff. What was wrong with that picture?"

Joe frowned, picturing the scene in the dark. "Biff was on the floor, for one thing. Okay, okay,"

he said, responding to his brother's look. "Chet had a black eye."

"Which was explained later," Frank said. "Logan clocked him one."

"There were book bags all over the place."

Frank nodded. "Also explained later. The Golden Boys grabbed them, and Biff was trying to get them back."

Joe was running out of things to describe in the scene. "Chet had the shovel in his hands," he finally said.

"And was there anything weird about the shovel?" Frank asked.

Joe shook his head. "You got me there."

"Think for a moment," Frank said. "Close your eyes and try to remember what you saw."

Joe tried. Then he opened his eyes and shrugged. "It was a shovel."

"But it was missing something," Frank insisted.

Joe tried to visualize the tool again. "It had a handle and a big, square tip. Probably used to shovel coal into the old furnace."

"Which meant it was probably lying around for years," Frank said. "Remember how it was down there? Anything in that basement would get dirty and dusty pretty fast."

"Including us," Joe had to admit. Then he saw what Frank was getting at. "But that shovel wasn't dirty."

"And it had only one set of fingerprints on it," Frank put in. "Kind of odd for a tool that must have been used a lot."

Joe's voice became eager. "But not so odd if somebody had cleaned up the thing."

"Which had to have happened *before* Chet got his prints on it," Frank finished triumphantly. "And there's only one reason I can think of to wipe a shovel clean."

"Someone wanted to get rid of his fingerprints," Joe agreed. "The same person who used the shovel on poor Biff."

He began to get really excited. "Hey, we've got to talk to the Mortons. This is proof that Chet didn't do it."

"I was thinking of trying it on Con Riley," Frank said. "It might open a whole new avenue of investigation for them."

Joe punched the air. "Let's do it!"

Together, they moved to the exit. Frank was surprised at how dark it had grown since he'd gone in.

The open door threw a shaft of light on to the van. In the front seat, Callie looked up from the book she was reading and waved.

"You didn't tell me Callie was coming along," Joe said.

"Yeah, well, we'll drop her at her house before we go and talk with Con." Frank walked out to the parking lot.

He glanced around to check out the sunset. It was mainly blocked by the bulk of the school. But he could make out a few streaks of glowing purplish red behind the scaffolding for the Seneca sign.

A quick movement on the scaffolding caught his eye—a head, ducking down!

Frank couldn't make out any features. The head was silhouetted against the dying sunlight.

Frank lost interest until he saw the piece of lumber come flying down.

He got ready to dodge, then realized the two-by-four would miss him by yards.

It wasn't aimed at him.

The big, heavy piece of wood was aimed at the van—and Callie!

11 Big Break

Joe Hardy followed his brother's horrified gaze. Instantly, he realized where the piece of lumber was going to land.

"Callie!" both boys called out at almost the same time.

She won't see that thing coming down, Frank thought. Not till it's too late.

"Callie!" Frank yelled, now frantic. "Move!"

Callie bailed from her seat and flew into the back of the van.

At the same second, the whole van shuddered as the two-by-four smashed through its windshield. A webwork of cracks spread through the glass around the quivering board. Then the whole windshield sagged in, separating into about a million pieces.

Frank ran forward, shouting Callie's name.

Joe whipped around, keeping an eye on the roofline of the building. If anyone sent more surprises flying down, he'd be ready to give warning.

A moment later the van's engine roared to life. "I'm pulling back to the far end of the lot," Frank called through the now-open windshield.

"Good idea," Joe said. Nobody would be able to throw stuff that far.

Joe walked backward away from the school building, still watching for any movement from the roof above.

Nothing. Whoever had tossed that beam must have hit and run.

Still backing up, Joe reached the parking lot fence. Then he went to catch up with Frank and Callie in the van. He looked through the space where the windshield had been.

Frank knelt by the backseat, his arm around Callie. Although she seemed pretty shaken up, she still managed a joke. "Chased by a car. Now attacked by a board. I tell you, Hardy. Dating you is never boring."

While Frank and Callie talked quietly, Joe checked out the damage. There were a lot of rounded glass pellets scattered across the front seats.

Joe dug out the brush they used to get snow off the windshield. Now I'm using it to brush up the

windshield he thought, sweeping the glass into a garbage bag. Then he went to work getting the glass off the floor.

He pulled out the floor mats to shake them into the bag. That was when Joe discovered the floor of the van had a good-size dent in front of the passenger seat.

That must be where the board landed, Joe thought. They were lucky—both the engine and the controls had escaped damage. He decided not to mention the dent until Callie left. It was right where her legs would have been if she hadn't moved.

At last Frank came around to get behind the wheel. Joe took the passenger seat. Not surprisingly, Callie decided to stay where she was.

Frank took side streets and kept the speed down. Even so, Joe had the strange experience of feeling a breeze full in the face as they rolled along. "So this is the wind we're supposed to be shielded against," he said. "It's a little like riding in a convertible."

Callie laughed. "A convertible van. There's an idea."

"I'd prefer a normal, boring van if you don't mind," Frank told them.

When they arrived at Callie's house, Frank walked her to the door.

"Is she okay?" Joe asked when Frank came back.

"Except for the death grip she kept on my arm, I'd say yes." Frank flexed his arm a couple of times, as if he were trying to get the blood flowing again. "Probably end up with a bruise there." He put the key in the ignition and started the engine. "Where to now? Home or Con Riley?"

"If you think we can get downtown, let's talk to Con," Joe decided.

They drove in silence for a few minutes, then Joe spoke up. "Maybe we should have taken that email threat a little more seriously. Whoever sent it certainly underlined his point with that two-by-four."

But Frank shook his head. "Those were two different things. The threat and computer virus—those were intellectual." He nodded toward the windshield. "Breaking that was very physical."

"So you're saying the message came from the brainy kids."

"Smashing our windshield was a message, too," Frank said. "A very direct message."

"But something more like what you would expect from a jock," Joe said. He fell silent. "It's almost as if the jocks and the nerds are working together. But why would the debate kids help the guys who were terrorizing them?"

Frank shrugged, still keeping his hands on the wheel. "Maybe because they're still terrorized," he suggested.

He frowned for a moment, thinking. "Or try this on for size. As long as what happened to Biff is a big mystery, the football team is getting a lot of attention. Not to mention suspicion. People like Old Beady Eyes and Coach Devlin will be watching."

"Yeah," Joe said, remembering the coach's locker-room speech. "So Golden and his boys can't act as they please anymore."

"Not without getting into serious trouble," Frank agreed. "Yeah. That's probably the last thing Terry Golden wants right now. I bet the college coaches who've been checking him out so eagerly have suddenly stopped calling."

Joe laughed out loud at that thought. "Couldn't happen to a nicer guy."

They parked on a side street near police head-quarters. Walking into the building, Frank asked for Con Riley. A few minutes later the Hardys stood in front of the police officer's desk.

Con gave them a guarded look. "To what do I owe the honor?" he asked.

Frank grinned. "We're calling it the mystery of the filth that wasn't."

"Maybe you recall we spent a little while in the school basement," Joe said. "We ended up covered in coal dust. As a matter of fact, everything down there was covered in coal dust."

"Except for the shovel in Chet's hands," Frank put in. "It was surprisingly clean."

Joe took his turn. "Like somebody wiped it off before Chet picked it up? Somebody who'd already used it?"

Con glanced around at the other officers working around him. Then he leaned forward. "You make a point," he said, keeping his voice low. "The same question was raised here. There should have been crud and other fingerprints on that shovel."

He shook his head. "On the other hand, the Morton boy was standing over the victim with the blasted thing in his hands. The D.A. was under pressure to charge someone as soon as possible, and I'm afraid Chet was the easy choice."

"But—" Joe began.

"The point you're making may become important at the trial," Con went on quietly. "It won't change the course of our investigation—such as it is."

"What's that mean?" Frank said equally quietly.

"It means a bunch of high-school kids are giving us the runaround," Con said in disgust. "We've collected a bunch of gossip and wild tales from students who probably weren't involved. But the ones we suspect were actually down in the basement have apparently gone deaf, dumb, and blind."

"Stonewalling," Joe said.

Con nodded. "That's it in a nutshell. The chief

wants us to be very careful. After all, we're dealing with honor students and football heroes."

The police officer looked as if he'd bitten into something rotten. "The media will be all over us if we press these kids too hard. But being polite and low-key has gotten us nothing so far. A big, fat zero."

"Have you talked to Mr. Sheldrake?" Frank suggested.

"The school authorities are getting nowhere, too. There are a dozen students. Put the screws to all of them, and it looks excessive. But unless we go that route, none of them will crack."

Con shrugged. "Ah, well. If we're lucky, we may not have to worry about that."

"What do you mean?" Frank asked.

"I probably shouldn't say this." Con glanced around again. "But I think I can depend on you two to keep your mouths shut. There's been some good news from the hospital."

"About Biff?" Joe said excitedly.

"Keep your voice down, son!" Riley hissed.

He lowered his own voice again. "Discussing the case, the doctors have stopped talking about *if* Biff will regain consciousness. It's become *when.*"

Joe smiled. "So, sooner or later, you'll be able to ask Biff what happened."

Con nodded. "And when that happens, I expect a lot of people may be changing their stories."

Frank looked thoughtful. "So you still may be able to clear this up without taking Chet to court," he said.

"Let's just say I'm not a hundred percent convinced the boy is guilty," Con replied.

"We've got a little mystery of our own," Frank said. "Which may happen to tie in with yours."

He explained what had happened outside the school.

Joe stared in surprise. He hadn't expected Frank to report the incident to the police.

Con's face grew red as he listened. "That was a very stupid stunt for someone to pull," he said angrily. "The Shaw girl could have been seriously injured."

He looked at the boys. "Do you want to make an official complaint?"

"Would it do much good?" Joe asked. "If you catch somebody—which right now is a big if— they didn't actually hurt anyone. From what I've seen, kids seem to get off pretty lightly when the cases go to court."

Con nodded silently, a little embarrassed. "But it might throw a good scare into whoever did it."

"Except we only have suspicions about who that was," Joe said. "Unless you're going to fingerprint that board—"

"There's an idea," Frank suddenly broke in.

Joe stared at his brother again. "I was joking!"

"Well, I think fingerprints and throwing a good scare might work well together." An evil smile slowly stretched his lips as he leaned toward the police officer.

"An official complaint probably won't get us very far. What I'd like, Con," he said, "is a little unofficial help. If you can give it . . ."

12 Cracking the Wall

Joe and Frank rode in the rear of the police cruiser.

This wasn't the first time Joe had found himself back there. He never liked it, though. Yes, civilians sometimes wound up in the back of patrol cars—crime victims, observers from the press, important people on inspections.

The backseat was usually reserved for criminals, though. Joe always got a feeling of being caged whenever he sat here.

There was also the faint perfume of low-life in the air. Drunks had probably barfed all over this seat.

Almost unconsciously, Joe found himself rub-

bing his fingers together. Give me some nice, clean coal dust any day, he thought.

Sitting in the front seat, Con Riley must have caught Joe's expression. "I got the cleanest car I could," he assured the boys. "Believe me. We give these babies a good going-over."

The smell of disinfectant was thick when the boys had gotten in, which made Joe wonder what they'd had to clean away.

Perhaps to take their minds off the smell, Con went into a war story. "Worst stink we ever had in a car happened when I was just starting out. Oh, it was awful—like rotting flesh! My partner and I were going crazy. We cleaned the backseat so much, they had to put a new cover on."

Joe couldn't help himself. "And?" he asked.

"Turned out it came from *under* the front seat." Con laughed. "A guy from one of the other shifts had stashed a liverwurst sandwich down there and forgotten about it. After a couple of weeks—"

"Con!" Frank Hardy interrupted in a strangled voice. "Do you think you could open these windows an inch or two?"

It wasn't a long drive, and soon the car pulled up in front of Wendell Logan's house.

"I hope you're right about this," Joe muttered as they got out and walked toward the house, leaving Con in the cruiser.

"I think we've got our guy," Frank said. "Whoever slung that beam around had to be big and strong. He also had to be the type who acts first and thinks later."

"That certainly fits our pal Wendell," Joe said.

"We've even got a motive. I expect he was pretty steamed at the way you handled him tonight in the locker room."

Joe shook his head. "Better me handling him than Logan manhandling *me*."

They were at the door, so Frank rang the bell.

Wendell's mother answered. "Hello, boys."

"Hi, Mrs. Logan. Could we see Wendell for a moment?" Frank asked.

Mrs. Logan glanced at her watch. "We were just about to sit down to dinner."

Frank raised his hands. "It will just take a couple of minutes, I promise. We'll wait for him here."

"All right." Mrs. Logan headed back inside. "Wendell!" she called.

A moment later a scowling Wendell Logan appeared at the door. "What do you two want . . ." The big guy's voice trailed off.

As the door opened, Con Riley started up the red flasher on top of the patrol car. In the blinking red light, Logan's face went a little pale.

"Ever hear of fingerprints, Wendell?" Frank Hardy asked.

"Some interesting ones turned up on the board

111

that trashed our windshield," Joe said. "Interesting enough that the cops want a set of yours."

"They may even try comparing them to a couple of partial prints on the shovel that was used to whack Biff Hooper," Frank put in.

Wendell Logan's rough, tough, bully mask slipped big-time. Now he just looked like a scared kid.

"I just meant for that board to land near your van!" he said. "I didn't think it would go that far!"

"That seems to be your problem in life," Joe said. "I bet you didn't mean to go as far as you went with Phil Cohen when you wound up knocking him down the stairs."

"There was a girl in the front seat of the van," Frank said grimly. "You're just lucky she wasn't hurt. Otherwise, that cop would be taking you in for assault."

Now Wendell Logan's face began looking a little green.

"Know what this makes me wonder?" Joe said. "Could things have gone a little too far in the furnace room? I saw the way you were looking at Biff after he helped me out on the stairway. Maybe you saw Biff helping those debate nerds and reacted the same way. For a big guy like you, all it would take was one swing—"

"No! I—I didn't do it!" Tears began to well up in the big guy's eyes. He was almost babbling.

"You know how those big brains always look

down on us. Some of the guys on the team just wanted to shake them up. And, yeah, Terry wanted a piece of Dan Freeman." The flood of words stumbled for a moment. "Me—I was hoping for a shot at Morton. I give a hundred and ten percent for the team, but everyone likes him better."

Maybe that's because, unlike you, he doesn't throw his weight around, Joe thought.

"Anyway, I knew where he'd be. He thought we were just going to jump out and scare the nerds a little. I got in one good punch, but then I lost him in the dark."

Wendell leaned forward, no longer looming. He had a pleading expression on his face. "But don't you see, I was *after* him. I couldn't have gotten to the furnace room *ahead* of him."

Joe wasn't so sure of Logan's argument. Remembering the maze of passages, he thought it was quite possible for someone to get turned around, running through the dark. A pursuer could take a different route and actually get in front of the guy he was chasing.

On the other hand, Joe had to believe that they'd cracked Wendell Logan's tough-guy front. Either he was telling the truth about not hitting Biff, or he was a tremendous actor.

Frank took the direct approach. "So who do you think did it?"

"I don't *know!*" From the way the words burst

from Logan's lips, it was obvious he'd been asked the question too many times. The look in his eyes showed he'd been thinking a lot about it, too.

"I've tried to go over the whole thing. Who was down in the basement—and where they were," he admitted, rubbing a big hand over his forehead as if the effort made his brain hurt.

"And what did you come up with?" Frank wanted to know.

"The best thing would be to say one of the nerds got Biff." Logan's lips twitched in disgust. "But they're all such wimps! I can't imagine one being able to pick up a shovel, much less swing it at somebody."

"But that would mean it was somebody from the team," Joe said.

Logan frowned and wouldn't or couldn't meet their eyes. "Yeah," he agreed. "The problem is, things were so confused down there. I know where I started out—I was right beside Terry. But after that, well, we were running around, chasing people."

He threw his arms out in different directions. "This way, that way . . . it was dark, and you know how everything is interconnected down there. Hallways lead into rooms that lead into other hallways."

"So you don't even know where Terry Golden was?" Joe pressed.

Logan still looked down, but his expression was

scared. "I—I couldn't tell you. We split up when I went after Chet. Next time I saw Golden, he was telling us to get out of there."

"When was that?" Frank asked. "And why?"

Logan shrugged. "He said he heard somebody talking about the cops. We were out of there fast! I was blocks away when I heard the sirens."

The Hardys looked at each other. Frank had sent Joe to get an ambulance *and* the police. The door to the furnace room had been open. If Terry Golden heard that, he'd been close to the scene where Biff was downed.

It looks like Logan suspects Golden, but he has no proof, Joe thought. There's nothing more to get out of him now.

Frank and Joe returned to the police car, and Con turned off the flasher. He gave the boys a lift back to their car.

While they rode, Frank and Joe passed along what Logan had told them.

Joe could see Con's face in the rearview mirror. The officer was frowning.

"That's a little more than we got," Con had to admit. I'm afraid it still doesn't tell us much, though."

"Just makes it a little easier for the guys to play dumb," Frank said. "Everything was so confused down there, they really don't know who was doing what."

115

"Whoever hit the Hooper boy knew what he was doing." Con's voice was grim.

"Did he?" Frank asked. "Think about it. You're chased through the dark, stumbled across a weapon, and grabbed it up. Somebody suddenly appears. You swing—"

"That's pretty much the way certain people figured it for your friend Chet," Con pointed out.

"It also seems to say that one of the people being messed with swung the shovel," Joe said. "Logan didn't think that was likely."

He hated what he was about to say, but it had to come out. "But somebody from the team could have handled that shovel. I think Logan—and maybe some of the other Golden Boys—are afraid that Terry Golden did it."

"That would be one explanation for the way they're all hanging together," Riley said.

"Or it could be that they're all scared about being punished," Frank put in.

"At least we know where two of those kids started out," Con said.

"And maybe where one ended up," Joe stubbornly added. "If Golden was warning people about the cops coming, that means he heard Frank and me talking. And it means he was near the furnace room."

"If he's the one who took Biff out, he'd be thinking of cops anyway," Frank said.

"Now, where exactly are you parked?" Con asked before they could get into an argument. By now they'd reached downtown Bayport.

Con shook his head when he saw the gaping hole where the windshield should have been. "You fellas be careful getting this thing home, now," he warned. "Do you want me to drive ahead?"

"Just what we need," Frank muttered as he got out. "A parade."

"I don't think we need a police escort, thank you, Con," Joe said. "We'll just take it easy."

Con nodded and wished the boys good night.

Frank got back behind the wheel. Joe took the passenger's seat. Soon they were heading for home.

"We probably should have called home," Frank said, flipping on the headlights. "I hope the folks aren't getting nervous."

Joe didn't answer.

"What's the problem?" Frank asked.

"You were pretty quick to dump on what I was saying to Con," Joe complained. "I didn't like your suggesting that it could be somebody from the team."

Frank gave him a look. "No, but you liked accusing Terry Golden."

"He's a two-faced sleaze who likes to blindside people," Joe replied hotly. "You've seen it, and I've been on the receiving end. And, no, I didn't think

117

it was such a bad idea to get that fact out there."

Frank looked ready to give Joe an argument. But he broke off, peering into the rearview mirror.

"Funny," he said. "The car behind us turned off the road."

"What's the big deal about that?" Joe was still ready for that argument.

"Look where we are." Frank gestured out through the nonexistent windshield.

He'd been taking a quiet route home, and this section was downright dead. Joe knew the area. The proper name was Fennerman Boulevard. But everyone called it Fenderbender Alley. The street was lined with cheap auto-body shops, and behind those, junkyards.

It was a good place to go if you needed to replace a fender, a door, or if your old car lost a hubcap. But that was basically a daytime business. "Midnight auto shop" generally had another meaning—a place where stolen cars were chopped up to be sold as parts.

Still, it wasn't midnight. Maybe somebody was just looking for a part after work.

Joe silently shook his head. And even if there are car thieves on the prowl, he thought, we've got enough other stuff to worry about right now.

"What kind of car was it?" he asked.

Frank shrugged. "The headlights were pretty high off the ground," he said. "A small truck, I

guess. Maybe an SUV I only noticed because he took a quick right."

They took the next block in silence.

The neighborhood *is* quiet, Joe thought. Without the windshield, you can hear everything. Except there's barely anything to hear.

A light breeze brought them the angry barking of a junkyard dog. Then Joe caught the sound of a revving engine and the squeal of tires. The noise came from around the corner and off to their right.

Funny, Joe thought. I'm not seeing the beams of any headlights.

They rolled into an intersection, and he turned to look behind him. Bayport's town government wasn't about to waste streetlights in this dead area. Joe had to squint as he peered back down into semidarkness.

The engine noise was loud, close . . . and coming closer.

Then he made out the shape of the big dark SUV roaring up to ram them!

13 Bumper Cars

"Gun it!" Joe yelled. "That guy's trying to ram us!"

Frank had heard the other engine. He just hadn't been able to make out where it was coming from.

At Joe's warning, he hit the gas pedal. Sudden acceleration pushed the boys back in their seats as the van leaped across the intersection.

An instant later a large black shape flew past the rear of the van.

"Missed us," Frank said, looking in the rearview mirror. "What kind of idiot pulls a stupid stunt like—"

His words were cut off by the sound of tires against pavement.

The SUV was revving up to try again. The big

vehicle wobbled from side to side, almost fishtailing as it pulled forward.

"Looks like he's the kind of nut to come after us," Joe said in a tight voice.

Frank didn't wait around to see what the mystery driver wanted. He gunned the engine and worked on getting out of there.

His face and Joe's were buffeted by the sudden breeze blowing in the open front of the car.

Can't go too fast, Frank thought, or it will be like trying to look into a gale. I won't be able to see where I'm going.

The driver behind them didn't seem to have a problem with speed. His front bumper thumped against the van's rear, jarring both boys.

"Can you see who's driving that thing?" Frank fought to hold the wheel as the van was rocked again.

"You think we'll recognize him?" Joe asked.

"I'd bet on it." Frank darted the van to the right, keeping the SUV from passing them.

Joe spent a long moment staring into the rearview mirror, then he shook his head. "It's got one of those tinted windshields," he finally said. "I can't see inside."

Frank sent the van squealing left to cut off their pursuer again. "Wish I could get inside there," he muttered. "I'd rap that clown on the head a couple of times."

He cut off as the SUV suddenly pulled up beside them. It bounced along, one side of its wheels up on the sidewalk.

"Brace yourself," Frank warned, matching the monster truck's speed. They bombed down the block as if they were one piece of metal.

That seemed to be what the driver of the SUV had in mind. He kept cutting the wheel to the left, banging against the van with bone-jarring force.

Joe felt himself flung against his shoulder belt one, two, three times.

If this guy gets ahead of us, it's all over, he thought. He'll force us into a wall—or a crash.

A thunderous impact made him cringe in his seat, thinking the worst had happened. No, it was just the juggernaut beside them ramming into a metal garbage can. The trash can flew up across the front hood of the SUV, bounced on the roof of the van, then disappeared behind them.

The screech of brakes filled the air, and the dark vehicle suddenly fell behind, fishtailing down the street.

Joe saw why—there was a lamppost ahead. If their pursuer had kept his course, he'd have crashed into it.

Then Joe was flung against the door as Frank made a sudden left.

"What—" Joe started to say as the van quickly picked up speed. This wasn't a breeze tugging at

his hair. He felt as if he were being smacked in the face by an unfriendly wind.

"Shortcut to the interstate," Frank explained. His eyes squinted against the wind whipping against his face.

"You're not getting on—" Joe began.

The roar of an abused engine cut him off. They'd swung onto a wider street. The SUV was pulling up again, trying to cut them off.

This time it came up on their left. They raced along, side by side, wheel to wheel, door to door.

Leaning into the wind, Joe looked past his brother. He hoped to get a glimpse of the mystery driver through the passenger-side window. But all the glass on the SUV was heavily tinted. A new burst of speed pushed Joe back in his seat. He still didn't have a clue as to who was behind the wheel of the SUV.

Joe couldn't tell how long that insane race went on. The next thing he knew, they were on the service road to the interstate.

His eyes were streaming from the chilly wind roaring in. How could Frank see where he was going?

Then, up ahead, Joe made out the entrance ramp to the elevated part of the roadway. It rose up to the left, while the service road remained at ground level on the right. Now Joe began to see what Frank had in mind.

A row of orange traffic cones led up to the split-off. The cones went flying or crunched under the tires of the dueling vehicles.

The driver of the SUV was desperately trying to get to the right, but Frank relentlessly herded him forward and to the left—even at the cost of some nasty knocks against the van.

They were almost to the split. The line of cones was just about gone. Ahead, a steel barrier rose up to divide the rising ramp from the ground-level service road.

Frank kept up the pressure on the SUV until Joe was convinced they were going to crash into the steel rail themselves. At the last moment Frank swerved away to the right. Luckily, there was very little traffic on the service road. Their lane was empty.

Their adversary wasn't so lucky. A big tractor-trailer rig was set on pulling onto the interstate. The huge truck was right on the tail of the SUV, its horns blaring. The driver who'd nearly wrecked them had no choice but to go up and away on to the interstate.

Sighing with relief, Frank slowed the van. They made the first possible turn to cut off of the service road and head for home.

Fenton Hardy wasn't happy to hear about what had happened that evening. "A windshield to be

replaced, plus who knows how many dents and scrapes?" He shook his head.

He didn't fool his sons. The boys knew their father was more worried about them—and Callie—than any repair costs.

"You know that SUV that followed us down to Fenderbender Alley," Frank said, "had to start tailing us when we switched from Con's patrol car to our van."

He looked at Joe. "Who knew we were in a patrol car heading downtown?"

"You, me, Con—and Wendell Logan." Joe scowled furiously. "And I bet I know who he told—Terry Golden!"

"Knowing it and proving it—" Fenton began.

"I think we should give Con a call about that SUV," Joe said, going to the phone.

"Golden doesn't drive one."

"No, but I'll bet you it will turn out that one was stolen not far from where he lives," Joe growled.

"Which is still—" Fenton said.

"I know, Dad—it's still not proof." Looking disgusted, Joe passed along his information. He listened for a moment, thanked Con, and hung up the phone.

"What do you know?" Joe said. "They just got a report of a late-model SUV disappearing on Ash Street. Golden lives on Beech, just a block away."

"No more detecting," Aunt Gertrude said, com-

ing out of the kitchen. "I've reheated your dinner. Sit down and eat."

After finishing his late dinner, Frank borrowed his father's computer to download the latest antivirus software update. Sure enough, the website had information about a mutated version of the Gravedigger bug.

Then came the tiresome business of booting-up his computer and trying to clean out the infected files. Some could be saved. Many, however, had to be erased.

Of course, one of the casualties was the program he'd been trying to write.

Frank was just finishing the job when Joe came pounding up the stairs.

He stuck his head into Frank's room. "The ten o'clock news just came on," he announced.

Frank looked up from the computer monitor. "So? Can't Aunt Gertrude answer her sports contest question?"

"That's not the news, judging from the top-of-the-hour headlines. Dad thought you'd want to see this for yourself."

They went downstairs. The now-familiar School Attack logo floated behind the blond news anchor.

"We have a startling new development to report in the case of Monday's school attack," the young

woman said. "Doctors at Bayport General have upgraded the victim's status. They expect Biff Hooper to make a full recovery."

She smiled into the camera. "The young man is expected to recover consciousness within the next few days. Perhaps when he does, he'll be able to explain exactly what was going on in the basement of Bayport High School. Sources within the police have admitted to BayNews that even though an arrest has been made, they still haven't gotten to the bottom of Monday's incident."

A commercial came on, and Joe shook his head. "Well, at least this time they didn't show poor Chet's picture."

Frank's face settled into a thoughtful frown. "It will be interesting to see how some people act in school tomorrow."

Actually, the school day turned out to be pretty boring. The two people Frank really wanted to see—Terry Golden and Dan Freeman—weren't in school.

Without the distraction of the case, Frank found himself settling into the flow of classes. He even managed to figure out one of Mr. Patel's trig problems.

Callie wasn't in class, either. When the end-of-school buzzer sounded, Frank gathered up his

books. Maybe I should stop by Callie's before I get the bus to the university, he thought. I can pass along the homework assignments and see how she's doing.

He was surprised to find his brother waiting for him outside the classroom.

"I decided to ditch practice today," Joe told his brother. "We have a visit we ought to pay—to Bayport General."

There goes my time with Callie, Frank thought. But he nodded, silently promising to make it up to her later. "I can't think of a better reason to be late for my computer class," he told Joe.

Luckily, the hospital was within walking distance. The van was already laid up for repairs.

Frank's nose wrinkled the minute they stepped into the hospital. Maybe it was his imagination, but he always felt the place had an unusual smell: recycled air, disinfectant, and sick people.

They got good news and bad news at the reception desk. Biff had been moved from the intensive care unit to a private room in the east wing. That meant his condition was definitely improving.

"But he's not being allowed any visitors," the receptionist went on. "Only his immediate family. The police even have a guard on the door!"

Joe covered his disappointment with a wisecrack as they turned away from the desk. "Sounds like

Chief Collig is overreacting to last night's scoop on the news."

As he spoke, a loud, insistent tone began bleating from what seemed like every intercom unit in the hospital.

Joe swung back to the receptionist. "What is that?"

The woman looked a little nervous. "That's the fire alarm. There weren't supposed to be any drills today—"

"Hey, maybe we'd better stick around and lend a hand," Joe suggested to Frank. "I bet there are a lot of people in here who can't move on their own." His eyes suddenly went wide. "Like Biff!"

"The hospital has plans to take care of emergencies like this," Frank pointed out. "You heard the lady—they practice for this sort of thing." He grinned. "What do you bet this whole production turns out to be an unannounced fire drill?"

His face grew more serious. "And even if it's not, the chances are the two of us would just be getting in the way."

They headed outside, into the afternoon sunlight. Frank checked his watch. "If I get lucky and catch a bus right away, I can still make my class."

Joe looked off in the direction of the school. "Coach Devlin won't be happy at my being late, but I suppose I could still turn up for practice."

They were about to go their separate ways when Joe suddenly grabbed Frank's arm. "Hey, what's that?"

"That" was something moving in one of the patches of bushes and trees that edged the hospital parking lot. Frank squinted. It looked like . . . a foot?

The Hardys quickly headed over to the patch of greenery. The moving object definitely was a shoe. And from the jerky motions it kept making, there had to be a foot inside. Apparently someone was lying under the bushes, trying to worm his way out.

Strange place to take a nap, Frank thought as they neared the shrubbery.

"Need some help?" Joe asked.

Their answer came as half a groan and half a moan.

The boys went to work pulling branches away from the body. Maybe the person had collapsed and fallen into the planted area. . . .

Frank gasped when he got a glimpse of the person's face. He recognized Dan Freeman—just barely.

Dan's face was battered and bloody. Both eyes had almost swollen shut. Dan looked up at them through bruised slits.

"We'd better get you to the emergency room," Joe said.

"Who did this to you?" Frank asked.

It took Freeman a moment to recognize them. Then he frantically started trying to push himself up.

"Golden! Golden . . . in the hospital!" he gasped. "Set a false alarm. He—he's trying to get Biff Hooper!"

14 Bad Medicine

Frank and Joe helped Dan up.

"Come on," Joe said, turning toward the emergency room entrance. "We'd better have a doctor look at you."

"Noooo!" Dan feebly began pulling them toward the main doors of the hospital. "Got to stop Golden. He's in there trying to kill Hooper!"

Sighing, Frank let Dan lead them. "I think you'd better go ahead," he told Joe. "Let the folks in the hospital know this may be a false alarm."

Joe took off, and Frank put an arm around Dan, helping him stay upright.

The tall, gangly boy was pushing his battered body way past its endurance point. He was gasping

for breath and wobbling by the time they made it through the doors.

The lobby of the hospital was a scene of chaos. Nurses were leading patients who could walk on their own out the doors. Some of them were helped—or hindered—by worried visitors.

Other people—healthy people—were pushing ahead. Frank shook his head in silent disapproval. Apparently, the discovery that this wasn't a drill had panicked them.

A heavyset older man, intent on getting to the exit, brushed past Frank and Dan. There really wasn't enough room for him. As he went by, the stranger's elbow caught Dan in the ribs.

The tall boy folded in half, almost collapsing. His breath came out as a thin whistle as he clutched at his rib cage. Frank tried to be gentle as he held Dan upright.

"That could be a cracked rib—or worse," he warned.

Man, he thought worriedly, Golden must really have worked him over.

"Dan," Frank said firmly, "you've got to see a doctor."

"No! We've got to find Golden!" Gritting his teeth, Freeman led Frank into the crowd.

"It's all my fault," Dan muttered. He looked at Frank. "I put Hooper in here."

Frank didn't know what to say. He'd always

thought of Dan as a possible suspect, even though Joe kept beating the drums for Terry Golden.

Dan nodded, his bruised face miserable. "Yeah. I was the one. Couple of other guys and I went after the goons who stole our books. As soon as we got into the basement, the punching began."

He took a deep, shaky breath. "I took one in the mouth and one in the gut but managed to break away in the dark. Then I was running through that maze down there. Wound up in the furnace room. It looked like a good place to hide. Tripped over something on the floor. . . ."

"The shovel?" Frank asked.

Freeman nodded in reply. "I'd just picked it up when the door flew open. All I saw was a big, hulking shadow coming past me. So I swung. I swung with all my might—"

He choked at the memory. "It was panic, and what I did next was panic, too."

"You wiped the shovel clean," Frank said.

"Thought I'd killed him," Dan gulped. "Always read a lot of mystery stories. "So I got rid of my fingerprints and got out of there."

He looked sick—far worse than he did from the effects of his beating. "But Golden saw me come out. He lost me in the dark again, but he was still searching when you and your brother came along. He heard you talking about the cops."

Dan took another long, shuddering breath.

134

Frank thought he had the next part of the story figured out. "When did Golden start blackmailing you? Did you mess up my computer because he told you to?"

"No, I did that on my own," Dan admitted, looking embarrassed. "You kept poking around, asking questions. I wanted everyone to forget about it."

"That wasn't going to happen," Frank told the other boy.

"Guess not," Dan said. "Should have realized that. But I couldn't get my brain in gear. Then, last night . . . Golden called me. He was in a panic. Said he'd done something to try to stop you."

"Oh, yeah," Frank said, remembering his auto duel with the SUV.

"And then the news said that Biff was going to wake up. The whole story would come out. Golden would lose his possibility for a football scholarship." Dan gulped again. "He said if he went down, I'd go down with him. The only way to stop that was to make sure Hooper didn't recover."

Frank saw the picture now. "So your job was to come up with a brilliant plan."

Dan nodded. "I remembered this murder mystery I'd read. The villain killed someone who was in a coma by injecting an air bubble into the intravenous drip."

Frank had read the same story. "So all Golden

had to do was dress up as a hospital aide and cause some distraction."

"It was all right so long as it was just a thought," Freeman said. "But when we came down here, and he was actually going to do it . . . I *tried* to stop him."

And got beaten bloody, Frank thought, looking at the boy he was helping to hold up. Dan's face was bruised and swollen. Smears of drying blood trailed around his nose and mouth.

"We were in his car—I couldn't get away." Freeman closed his eyes, as if he were trying to make the memories of his beating go away.

"I—I must have passed out," Dan said, opening his eyes again. "Next thing I knew, I was under those bushes. In the distance, I could hear a fire alarm going off. Then you and your brother found me."

The tall boy turned pleading eyes to Frank. "It's not just that Golden beat me. He dumped me like I was a sack of garbage. I know he's inside the hospital now, looking for Biff. We've got to stop him, Hardy. He's really out of his mind."

All the time they were talking, they'd fought their way against the tide of people trying to get out of the hospital. Frank noticed the reception desk was empty now.

Sure, he realized. The woman who was there probably has duties somewhere else during an emergency.

All the time they were fighting the crowd in the lobby, Frank had angled his and Dan's course. Now they reached the swinging doors that led to the east wing of the hospital.

The doors stood wide open, and the crowd in that area had begun to thin out. Those who could walk were out of the way.

Now the hospital staff could start moving the more difficult cases.

Freeman was slowing down, losing steam. Even his iron will couldn't keep his terribly injured body going.

He stopped talking, concentrating on taking one step, then another.

They were into the east wing before he turned suspicious eyes on Frank.

"You're not just taking me to some doctor, are you?" Dan demanded.

"No," Frank told him. "This is where they transferred Biff." He looked up and down the long hallway. "At least, his room is somewhere along here. They didn't give me the number, but we should be able to spot the police guard."

Dan stared at Frank. "Guard?"

Frank nodded. "Joe laughed at the idea when the hospital receptionist told us. I guess we should be glad for it now. Looks as though Chief Collig suspected something like what you and Golden cooked up."

Dan Freeman staggered as if Frank had punched him.

"I tried to stop it," he said in an agonized voice. "You've got to believe me!"

"I believe you," Frank said. "Those marks on your face would be impossible to fake." He sighed. "I just wish you hadn't started this whole thing in the first place."

He meant the crazy scheme to silence Biff. But Dan took it right back to the old furnace room.

"I thought he was one of the guys after me," he moaned. "Self-defense. I should have gone for help. But I thought it was too late."

Dan turned feverish eyes on Frank. "Then— then you told me that Hooper was actually trying to *stop* what was going on. I wanted to throw up. He was only trying to help us . . . and I almost killed him."

Dan was trembling so badly, he couldn't even put one foot in front of the other.

"We've got to sit you down," Frank said. "You're not in any shape to keep wandering around."

He saw a chair in an empty room. "There. You can sit for a couple of minutes while I find Biff's guard—"

"No!" Dan struggled weakly against Frank's supporting arm.

Frank was determined to steer the other boy to the seat. "You're just exhausting yourself, Dan.

I'll be able to move a lot more quickly on my own."

Dan suddenly froze. "There!" he said. "There he is!"

"What?" Frank turned to see a police officer backing out of a room about three doors down.

The officer was pulling one end of a wheeled hospital bed. A familiar figure lay still and silent under the covers—Biff Hooper.

Frank stared in dismay. He always thought of Biff as big and hearty, but his friend seemed to have shrunk somehow. And his face looked as white as the sheet drawn up to his neck.

One arm was out from under the covers. Frank could see the heavy-gauge needle slipped into Biff's pale flesh and taped in place. A transparent plastic tube ran from the needle to a wheeled stand. The tube ran through a beeping machine and then into a bag of clear fluid.

No, Frank corrected himself. It runs *from* the intravenous drip into Biff's arm.

He and Dan managed to take one step toward Biff when a man burst out of the room ahead of them.

The white-haired newcomer was wearing a patient's gown that flapped open at the back. It revealed spindly legs and a pale, mottled rear end as the man crouched over a metal walker.

"You're not going to leave me here to burn!" the

patient yelled, trying to balance himself and move forward.

The red-haired nurse moving Biff's IV machine looked up in alarm. "Mr. Krantz! You're not supposed to be out of—"

The patient definitely shouldn't have been out of bed. He was too weak even to pick up his walker. Instead, he pushed against the metal frame. It toppled over—and so did he.

The medical team that was moving Biff abandoned the bed as Mr. Krantz crashed to the floor. Even the cop went to help.

Under Frank's supporting arm, Dan Freeman's shoulders suddenly stiffened.

Frank's eyes went from the man on the floor to a spot farther down the hallway. He saw what had upset Dan so much.

It was the figure in the green gown. A guy with long blond hair.

Terry Golden.

The jock wasn't wearing his usual football-hero smile. His face looked as hard and set as stone.

Somewhere, he'd managed to get hold of a hypodermic needle.

And he was headed straight for the unconscious, helpless Biff. . . .

15 Last Down

"Go!" Dan Freeman said fiercely, pushing at Frank. He staggered when he lost the older Hardy's arm. But Dan still sent him forward.

Frank charged ahead in his best broken-field run. He darted around Mr. Krantz tangled in his walker, sidestepping the group of nurses and the kneeling cop.

"Golden!" Frank yelled. "The secret's out! There's no getting away with this. Don't be stupid. Give it up!"

But Terry Golden kept on coming.

Biff's bed—and its silent occupant—stood between them. It was like some sort of horrible race, some strange game where the goalpost had been transferred to the middle of the field.

Frank put everything he had into running. He passed Biff's bed while Golden had about two steps to go.

No time to pull anything fancy, Frank thought. He went for a plain tackle.

The two boys crashed together with bruising impact. Frank wrapped his arms around Terry Golden and held on for dear life.

Although he'd managed to check Golden, Frank hadn't fully stopped him. Golden was determined to keep going . . . and he was larger. Frank found himself knocked backward by the bigger boy's weight.

Frank hung on, pulling Golden with him. Even as they fell, he twisted so that Terry wouldn't be on top of him. Frank also shifted his grip.

His hands went from Golden's middle to the wrist of the hand holding the hypodermic needle.

They crashed to the floor right at the head of Biff's bed. Frank tightened his hold on Terry's wrist, smashing the hand with the hypodermic against one of the bed's wheeled legs.

Once . . . twice . . . the third time he smacked Golden's hand against the metal, Frank got lucky. The jock lost his hold on the needle. It clattered to the floor and rolled under the bed.

Yelling with rage, Terry Golden grabbed a handful of Frank's hair. He rammed Frank's head against the floor hard enough to make Frank see stars.

Frank was a little wobbly as he pushed himself up to his knees.

Golden was on hands and knees, too, half under the bed as he searched for the hypodermic needle.

Frank grabbed him around the waist and hauled him back. Golden tried to shove him off, pushing against the bed. The force of their struggle sent the hospital bed rolling forward about a foot. The intravenous tube pulled taut, and the attached machine began to beep.

The sound distracted Frank—he didn't see Terry Golden's fist flying for his face.

He felt it, though. That punch knocked him off his knees, causing him to land flat on the floor.

Then Golden was all over him, hammering him with both fists, his face wild.

This must have been what happened to Dan, Frank thought as he twisted and tried to block the worst of the blows. He was at a definite disadvantage. Golden was on top, straddling his chest. Gravity was on the side of every punch the jock threw.

Frank twisted his head so that Golden's latest punch just skimmed the side of his head and smashed into the unyielding floor.

Golden yelled, relaxed his fist, and tried to shake the pain away. Frank grabbed with both hands, catching several of Terry's bruised fingers, pulling and twisting them.

The unexpected attack caught Golden by surprise. Frank flung himself around and sent his enemy toppling to the floor.

But when he tried to jump onto Golden and subdue him, Frank felt a foot in his chest. He flew backward, crashing into the corridor wall. Biff's bed stood several feet away as Frank pushed himself up. Golden was much closer.

If he goes for that hypo again— Frank thought.

Instead, Terry Golden staggered to his feet, pulling himself up on the rolling intravenous stand.

He looked around wildly as if searching for a weapon. Then he found one—the heavy metal stand he was clinging to.

Golden was tall, and he had muscles. Even so, he grunted as he brought the stand around to waist level. The machine's warning beeps turned into a shrill alarm as Golden reared back to swing the weighted base down on Biff.

"Golden!" Frank wheezed. "It's no good. You can't get away!"

One look at Golden's face showed him that the jock was too far gone to think anymore. He'd come to silence Biff Hooper, and that's what he'd do, no matter how many witnesses saw him. No matter what the consequences might be.

Frank readied himself for a hopeless leap. He was just too far away.

And then Golden was stumbling, the IV stand flying from his hands to crash to the floor. Frank's eyes went from Golden's face to his feet, where a bruised Dan Freeman clung tenaciously to the jock's ankles.

Terry Golden howled like a frustrated animal, kicking at Dan. But Frank was on his feet now and closing fast. His fist caught Golden on the point of his chin, hammering him back.

Golden went down on his back, away from the hospital bed and its helpless patient. He tried to pull himself up, but Frank knocked him flat with a body block. Even so, Golden struggled, screaming and clawing.

Now Frank had him down and kept him down.

And then the police guard was pounding up the corridor, his pistol drawn. . . .

"Sounds like I missed a whole bunch of excitement." Biff Hooper's voice was very, very quiet in the hospital room.

It was four days after the wild fight on the floor of the east wing. Two days had passed since Biff had opened his eyes and come out of his coma.

Joe Hardy grinned. "Yeah, a couple of things happened during your relaxing nap."

He and Frank were Biff's first nonfamily visitors. After hearing what had happened, Biff had demanded that he see them.

145

He shifted in his bed to look at Frank. "Looks like Golden managed to land a few on you," he said.

Frank grimaced, then winced. He carried quite a few bruises from Terry Golden's wild barrage of blows.

"If you think Frank looks bad, you should see Dan Freeman." Joe shook his head. "Put Dan and you side by side, and he'd make *you* look healthy."

That brought a grin to Biff's pale face. Although the worst was past, he still faced a long recovery.

"And you managed to miss the big fight completely," he said to Joe.

"I did consider taking a swing at a couple of hospital administrators." Joe couldn't keep the disgust out of his voice. "They were still giving me the why-should-we-listen-to-some-punk-kid routine when the cop told them to call for backup.

"That's all we'd have needed," Frank burst out. "The cop wasn't sure who was up to what. He wanted to arrest all of us."

"Con Riley straightened things out when he arrived," Joe said. "By then the hospital folks realized Terry wasn't an employee."

Frank nodded. "And then there was the hypodermic needle with his fingerprints all over it. Not to mention poor Dan telling the whole story."

Biff got more serious. "Sounds as though he took some pretty bad lumps stopping Golden."

"I hope it does him some good," Frank said.

"You mean if he gets charged for swinging that shovel on me?" Biff said. "I've spent some time thinking that over, and I don't blame Dan. He thought he was defending himself."

"Yeah, but there are other charges, too," Frank said. "Hindering a police investigation. And he's the one who came up with the crazy scheme to shut you up—permanently."

"He also fought to stop it," Biff pointed out.

"Doing the right thing—even if it happened pretty late in the day," Frank said, "that could keep him from doing jail time." He shook his head. "Dan's getting punishment enough. All the top colleges that were so interested in him . . . well, they're a lot cooler on him now."

"So his big plans have gone up in smoke," Biff said.

"Just like Terry's football career," Joe put in.

"I don't know about that," Biff said. "Look at some of the people in the NFL."

"You mean the National Felons League?" Joe joked. "Even so, I don't know that many colleges that would be happy with his unnecessary roughness."

They sat in silence for a few minutes. Then Biff said, "You want to know the really weird thing? They were all worried about what I would say when I came to. But I never knew what—or who—hit me."

147

"You could have told the cops who was behind it all," Frank pointed out.

Biff made a face. "I knew Golden had something in mind for the basement, but I didn't know what—or when."

"Then Wendell Logan told you," Joe said.

"I thought I could stop it if I grabbed the bait— those books—and got those kids out of there." Biff sighed. "Maybe things would have been a lot easier if I'd just gone to Mr. Sheldrake."

"There was a time when *I* thought about talking with Old Beady Eyes," Frank said. "But I didn't want to get people in trouble. Including you."

Biff could only shake his head. "It amazes me that I went along with Golden as long as I did. He talked a good game, about being a team, being special—"

"So long as you kissed up to his big, fat ego," Joe said.

"And when I tried to pull myself out of the whole mess—I guess I wasn't thinking too clearly," Biff confessed.

"Seems like a lot of people were guilty of that," Frank said.

"Yeah—jocks *and* brains," Joe agreed. "This time around, everybody dropped the ball."

"I guess that's the difference between football and life," Frank said.

"I always thought the big difference was not having cheerleaders," Joe joked.

Biff laughed, gesturing at his bed. "Is being stuck in here the real-life version of getting benched?"

"Maybe you should complain about unnecessary roughness," Joe suggested, grinning.

Frank smiled to see Biff reviving with Joe's kidding around. "Hey, sometimes life plays rough. The best you can do is try to recover your fumbles."

Biff got serious again. "Like Dan Freeman."

"I was thinking of *you*," Frank said. "You showed you were one of the good guys—even if you took some lumps for it."

Joe gently punched Biff's shoulder. "Always glad to have you on our team, big guy—way to go!"

The Hardy Boys Mystery Stories

Available from MINSTREL Books

Foul Play

Star football player Terry Golden gave Chet Morton a big smile. "I couldn't help noticing you had something danger-ous on your lunch tray."

"D-dangerous?" Chet stuttered. He looked down at his tray as if he expected to find a bomb on it.

Golden pointed to the piece of chocolate cake. "I'm talking about that!" Golden leaned in and ground his thumb into Chet's cake.

Chet stared, his mouth hanging open. He looked as if he couldn't believe what was happening.

Chet began to come out of his trance. "Hey, you—"

"What are you going to do, fat boy?" Golden's sneer dared Chet to try something. "I've got *teachers* afraid to go up against me." He gave Frank and Joe a smug grin. "That's what happens when you go with a winner."